D1527914

⊸❀ *Thieves in Retirement*

Middle Eastern Literature in Translation

Michael Beard *and* Adnan Haydar, *Series Editors*

Thieves in Retirement

A NOVEL

Hamdi Abu Golayyel

Translated from the Arabic by Marilyn Booth

 Syracuse University Press

First Edition 2006
06   07   08   09   10   11   6   5   4   3   2   1

Originally published in Arabic as *Lusus mutaqa'idun*
(Cairo: Mirit lil-nashr wa'l-ma'lumat, 2002).

The paper used in this publication meets the minimum
requirements of American National Standard for Information
Sciences—Permanence of Paper for Printed Library Materials,
ANSI Z39.48–1984.∞™

Library of Congress Cataloging-in-Publication Data
Abu Julayyil, Hamdi.
[Lusus mutaqa'idun. English]
Thieves in retirement : a novel / Hamdi Abu Golayyel ;
translated from the Arabic by Marilyn Booth.—1st ed.
p. cm.—(Middle Eastern literature in translation)
ISBN 0–8156–0852–7 (cloth : alk. paper)
I. Booth, Marilyn. II. Title. III. Series: Middle East literature in
translation
PJ7808.J85L8713   2006
892.7'36—dc22   2006014517

Manufactured in the United States of America

Death is one of the options you always have before you as a simple means of eliminating whatever danger it is that you face. Death is the endpoint of every danger, and at the same time it's the exemplary way to make your peace with all those dangers out there. It's far more calming, for instance, to be flattened by a car, or by a stray bullet or a strong narcotic, than to be quaking on your feet before some particular peril.

Hamdi Abu Golayyel, born in 1968, lives in greater Cairo. He is the editorial director for the Folk and Popular Culture Series in the Mass/Public Culture Administration, Government of Egypt. He writes for the daily *al-Ittihad,* a newspaper in the United Arab Emirates. He has published two volumes of short stories, *Asrab al-naml* (Swarms of Bees; Cairo: Hay'at Qusur al-Thaqafa, 1997) and *Ashya' matwiyya bi-'anaya fa'iqa* (Items Folded with Great Care; Cairo: al-Hay'a al-misriyya al-'amma lil-kitab, 2000). *Lusus mutaqa'idun* (Cairo: Dar Mirit, 2002) is his first novel. He has also published a work of nonfiction, *al-Qahira: Shawari' wa-hikayat* (Cairo: Streets and Stories; Cairo: Maktabat al-usra, 2003). He lives with his wife and two young daughters, Hala and Dunya.

Marilyn Booth is associate professor in the programs in Comparative and World Literature and Women and Gender Studies at the University of Illinois Urbana-Champaign. She has translated numerous works of fiction and memoir from the Arabic, including *Disciples of Passion* and *The Tiller of Waters* by Hoda Barakat; *Leaves of Narcissus* by Somaya Ramadan; *The Open Door* by Latifa al-Zayyat; *Children of the Waters: Stories by Ibtihal Salem* (winner of the University of Arkansas Press Arabic Translation Prize); *Points of Compass* by Sahar Tawfiq; and *My Grandmother's Cactus: Stories by Egyptian Women.*

Contents

.

Translator's Acknowledgments

I was in Cairo during the annual February book fair in 2002 on the day Hamdi Abu Golayyel's novel *Thieves in Retirement* appeared. My friend and colleague Muhammad Badawi insisted that I attend a panel discussion on the novel at the fair that evening. I bought the book, read it into the morning's wee hours, and sought out Hamdi the next day, thereby undermining permanently what had been my consistent (and honest) response to writers in search of a translator: that I always take time to decide. I'm grateful to Muhammad for his insistence, and to Hamdi for his friendship, patience, and good humor at being pestered with questions. I also thank Sahar Tawfiq for her smart suggestions as a sister translator and the series editors, Michael Beard and Adnan Haydar, for their enthusiasm (and Michael for some felicitous turns of phrase). I am thankful as always to Mary Selden Evans for her fierce support of Arabic literature in translation, as well as for her personal supportiveness and cheer. Finally, I am delighted and grateful that Paul Cuno-Booth was willing not only to comb Burton's astounding *Anatomy of Melancholy* for a possible source of the citation herein, but also, and above all, to read the manuscript with the expert linguistic street eye of an adolescent guy.

Introduction

ON THE FRINGES OF CITIES (CAIRO)
AND LANGUAGES (ARABIC)

If you were to fly to Cairo tomorrow, you'd see that it has become a glitzy signifier of globalization in action. You would also see the other side of globalization: worsening poverty, devastating inflation, non-unionized labor, and local resistances to all of this, partly taking the form of an increasingly appealing Islamist movement. These developments can be traced back, at least partly, to the initiatives of Anwar Sadat, who acceded to Egypt's one-party-rule presidency after the death of Gamal Abdel Nasser (Abd al-Nasir) in 1970. Sadat's Infitah (Open Door) ushered in an age of multinational-directed and USAID-overseen economic projects in Egypt. The Nasser regime's attempts in the 1950s and 1960s to institute agrarian reform, land redistribution, state-subsidized industry, and free public education and to limit foreign capitalist enterprise severely were at least partially dismantled or curtailed, to be replaced, symbolically, by the enormous Coca-Cola sign on one of downtown Cairo's highest buildings at the time. Such artifacts on Cairo's polluted horizon evoke the ways that Egypt and Egyptians are negotiating daily with the transnationalized pressures of Middle Eastern economies and politics.

These rapid changes, which many Cairenes see as rending Egypt's social fabric, may be one reason for the popularity in Egypt now of novels and films constructed around a house or a building, fictions that through their structures highlight and question issues of community and communication. The "house novel" can juxtapose characters of diverse tempers and origins, showing up the arbitrariness of physical proximity in a world where all seems to shift constantly, but perhaps questioning the "naturalness"—and the composition—of "family" and of the affections that we like to think surround and maintain this ubiquitous social institution. Hamdi Abu Golayyel intensifies this vision not only by describing the inhabitants of a single Cairene dwelling but also by envisioning that dwelling through the eyes of an admittedly capricious narrator making his way in the intricate social scaffolding of a Cairo neighborhood, amidst its other comings and goings.

Another pressure emerged when the mounting labor exodus of Egyptians to wealthy Gulf states in the last quarter of the twentieth century was largely reversed, as those states experienced economic difficulty and the demands of their own populations for better employment. One legacy of the post-Nasser years has been the return of many Egyptians from the Gulf with newly Islamized viewpoints and money to spend—although "Islamization" cannot be seen as a purely imported phenomenon by any means. You would see the signs of this in Cairo as well, and not only in the greater numbers of women and men wearing "Islamic garb."

Over the years, the breathtaking linguistic inventiveness of local shop names has been worthy of note. In the 1980s, favorite languages, often combined, were French and English, and references spoke to secular and consumerist aspirations: Cheri Home, Deco-Suq. Now, while wealthy residential areas boast Louis Vuitton, in the fast-growing middle-class suburbs of Cairo, such as New Ma'adi, the shops are determinedly local and referentially faith-based: Mecca Burgers, Baqqalat al-salat (Prayer grocery).

Nasserism seems far in the past, considering these burgeoning shop signs. But in contemporary Egyptian Arabic literature, the legacy of Nasserism lives on. Writers continue to wrestle with this provocative legacy. The ideology and practice of Nasser run through today's literature thematically, in its preoccupations ranging from social justice to neocolonialism to the valences of secularism and of pan-Arab allegiances; and equally in its focus on the alienation of the self from sources of community. Linguistically as well, Nasser's voice remains strong, if contested by the often satirical use writers make of the slogans and articulated beliefs of that time. Nasserism, I would even venture to say, saturates today's fictional scene. But it does so as an echo, an often fleeting linguistic reference, a way of putting words together that disintegrates through the text, subject to the pressures of later literary as well as sociopolitical moments. Herein lies an enormous challenge to the translator, to encapsulate that history which runs through the contemporary Arabic novel in Egypt, to institute it in translation as the indigenous echo it is in the Arabic; to retain the overwhelming impact of Nasser on cultural production as well as on every other sector of social existence yet to also enact—to show rather than to tell—the disintegration of this voice (but also its persistence) in contemporary Arab culture, for better or for worse.

It is no wonder, in the rapid changes and intense pressures of today's life, that the "house novel"—focusing on the inhabitants of a particular built environment—has flourished in Egypt. Able to convey both sympathetic closeness and crowded alienation, human needs for connection and the hardships of overly populated spaces, such novels trace the intensities and shifts in Egypt's increasingly urbanized fabric. *Thieves in Retirement* came out at about the same time as *The Yacoubian Building,* a novel that has garnered much notice and that focused on the comings and goings of the disparate residents of a venerable downtown Cairo apartment building, a structure at the heart of the urban pulse.

Thieves in Retirement, to the contrary, explores the well organized but only apparently semi-chaotic society of Cairo's fringe neighborhoods. Erected without much planning beginning in the Nasser period (1954–1970), these neighborhoods have proliferated during the more recent Sadat and Mubarak eras, in which state socialism and central planning gave way to the "Open Door" policy, encouraging foreign investment, acceding to most World Bank "structural reform" demands, and combining strong controls on the populace with little control of the ways overseas investment is shaping the Egyptian economy. These forces are evident in the novel through their impact on the lives of its characters. Abu Gamal (and the name, echoing Nasser's own given name, resounds with post-Nasserist irony) has been able to house his grown sons and their wives, plus a few tenants, in a small family building in a Nasser-era suburb built for factory workers. But he was forced into retirement from the factory as "rationalization" took over. The history of the neighborhood is part of the story; and the documentation of this history is one of collective and individual memory, one of encounters shaped through colloquial dialogue.

Rather than focus on middle-class angst, as so many modern

Egyptian novels have, or on village society, but usually from the viewpoint of urban writers, this novel centers on a marginalized population, composed of various and shifting elements. It is narrated by a young man who, like the author, is of Bedouin origin and from a family that was obliged by the government, along with the entire Bedouin population, to settle in government-designated residential clusters. Mingling his family's story with observation of the present from his vantage point as a tenant in Abu Gamal's dwelling, the narrator's construction of his relationship with Abu Gamal's sons and other tenants opens up a world of "local" (very local) justice, an underground economy based on drug dealing, and a social climate where ruthlessness and goodness seem hard to disentangle and sexual desire makes hash of a supposed public moral ambiance.

"Post-Nasserist" son Gamal is a consummate blend of customary belief with individualistic entrepreneurship in the underground economy and in an underground moral economy alike, all of his actions shaped through an institutionalization that shadows the official structures of society and yet shows the state as a fragile house of cards. The "son of Gamal" is a shadow Sadat, and all of the sons partake of a patriarchal relationship invoked through Nasserist vocabulary. At the same time, the novel offers a send-up of the diction of religiously sanctioned authority and of the languages of traditional conventional literary expression, best represented in poetry. "Professor Ramadan's" use of belletristic clichés to buttress his authority collides with Abu Gamal's very colloquial diatribes.

Equally, the juxtaposition of different levels of language collapses official narratives into vernacular ones. Told in a voice of ironic detachment yet also of affection, the novel explodes narrative conventions as the narrator chooses at various points whether to "act" as a character within the novel or to take the easier path of remaining at a circumspect narratorial distance, thereby satirizing the conventions of realist fiction that have governed fictional representation in Arabic literature until very recently. There is much humor in this novel, but much darkness as well; fear of the arbitrariness of life and of the ambiguity and inability to know the future shapes the narrator's search for security and all the characters' search for mutual respect in a social milieu that offers little of either. The text exploits and explicates customary notions of Bedouin "honor" and social organization, grafted onto wild urbanization.

The narrator is both uncitified Bedouin and polished urban speaker, simultaneously construction worker, café habitué, and sly storyteller. The novel's intricate language, seemingly simple, integrating colloquial phrases and proverbs into "literary" Arabic, is founded on a network of double meanings, puns, and references to the language of Nasserism, but the story is enacted on the level of individual and family life. Thus, the allegorical level of the novel is constructed through a second level of meaning even on the individual level of lexicon as well as in metaphor, as signaled in the novel's very title, *Thieves in Retirement.* Sentences proliferate at "crossroads," or rather "bifurcations," where a single word leads in two different directions, much as the narrator's choices govern the action. Characters and spaces personify each other. The novel satirizes the languages of "high" literary production as well as those of Nasserist and post-Nasserist ideologies, partly by dwelling on marginalized population groups that have been simultaneously romanticized and excluded by those discourses.

This novel seems emblematic of a new stage in contemporary Arabic literature. A new generation of writers, men and women, is melding attention to issues of socioeconomic right, gender politics, globalization (in all of its many forms), and dislocation with a profoundly introspective layering that eschews the navel-gazing of which some young writers over the past fifteen years have been accused, if not always with justification.

Thieves in Retirement is at the forefront of new Arabic literary creativities. Indeed, although the author is young and has published relatively little thus far, he has been hailed by critics as an important new voice. Indeed, he has won three literary prizes in the region, and a master's thesis has already been written on this novel in France.

Hamdi Abu Golayyel is of Bedouin origin, like his narrator, and he moved to Cairo from a settlement like the one he describes here. He writes for the daily *al-Ittihad,* a newspaper in the United Arab Emirates and has published two volumes of short stories, *Asrab al-naml* (Swarms of Bees; Cairo: Hay'at Qusur al-Thaqafa, 1997) and *Ashya' matwiyya bi-'anaya fa'iqa* (Items Folded with Great Care; Cairo: al-Hay'a al-misriyya al-'amma lil-kitab, 2000). *Lusus mutaqa'idun* (Cairo: Dar Mirit, 2002) is his first novel. He has also published a work of nonfiction, *al-Qahira: Shawari' wa-hikayat* (Cairo: Streets and Stories; Cairo: Maktabat al-usra, 2003). Abu Golayyel is the recipient of three literary awards: Ja'izat al-majmu'a al-qisasiyya (Award for a Short Story Collection), Ministry of Culture, Egypt, 1997; Ja'izat al-qissa (Award for Fictional Narrative: Short Story), *Akhbar al-yawm,* Cairo, 1999; and Ja'izat al-ibda' al-'arabi (Arabic Creative Writing Award), United Arab Emirates, 2000.

Through the narrative structures of their fictions, Abu Golayyel and other writers are embodying personal identity in the language of community critique and with subtle recourse to narratives of national history, questioning dominant narratives through the construction of subaltern perspectives. Just who *are* those "thieves in retirement"?

Marilyn Booth
Urbana, Illinois

Thieves in Retirement

1

Suppose that the life you think is your own, the life you are living at this very moment, is really the life of a character in some novel. And if that is so, then you can also see that this character is a slick exploiter of what you thought was your own knack for dodging the facts and telling tales. The guy also turns out to be really good at kissing up to people, even (and especially) when it's a case of people you take great pleasure in despising.

Once you can accept all these possibilities, though (and only then), you're free to step right into a rare experience with its own particular atmosphere, and it'll be an experience that you'll have every right to boast of. That's because the heroes of novels get to enjoy some astonishing antics that they would never get away with anywhere else. Anywhere beyond the edges of a sheet of writing paper that fell by chance—or perhaps not by chance—onto a table in front of a fellow whose full attention is on a very nicely stoked cigarette fortified by a glass of tea, though one presumably without sugar, since that's how intellectuals claim to drink their tea these days.

Here is a fellow who can't seem to fill the tedium of his days but by making up characters, even though they always come out flabby and exaggerated. Yet even these are worthwhile when it comes to solving your truly knotty problems (and how many they are). And they're skillful enough to launch themselves into some thrilling adventures awash with naked emotion whose scandalous exposure only the truly clever will appreciate. This will be the sort of escapade where you risk rubbing right up against your enemies, getting close to them, growing so fond of them, in fact, that even a passing greeting, the briefest of hand-clasps, turns into a momentous act that keeps its tight grip on your memory forever. For if you were able to watch yourself as you suck in a deep breath immediately after exchanging hellos with someone who makes your guts churn, you would find that you are oblivious to everything around you, having neglected—or, to put it better, scoffed at—trading handshakes with friends. Social niceties such as this tend to get lost quickly amidst the accumulation of duties we ceaselessly perform despite their burdensome nature.

This train of thought quickened my heart, because I felt it was pretty deep stuff, but it didn't cause me to quicken my lagging pace as I got near to our street. I was completely exhausted and in desperate need of a vacation, even a very short break, from playing the role of hero nonstop in my novel. And from smiling into all those faces, whether friend or foe.

I hope I won't see anyone.

I hope I won't run into Abu Gamal . . . lounging on his bamboo chair in front of the house as he's usually doing, in expectation of people's hellos. Things haven't been so great recently and I am not up to it. I'm not up to pulling together the show of delight and welcome I deluge him with on a daily basis, in a performance that's exactly as strong as my fear of the man.

Traffic was at a complete standstill today. Someone in charge of officially opening some new government project wanted to convince fellow citizens of its importance, I guess, so he stopped all traffic for the duration. It was a clever little ruse, actually, even though it exposed his scheme to a certain amount of verbal abuse expansive enough to include other projects and some well-known personalities. But the project's finer points did have the leading role on the tongues of everyone in the vicinity.

In any case, the truly upsetting things that were to confront me erupted only as a natural consequence of my own calamitous mistakes, which I'd kept well hidden until this day came to expose all of them scandalously.

From the age angle, Abu Gamal is the eldest resident of No. 36, and from the official angle, he is the owner of this building, unrivaled, more akin to a fortress: the bulging muscles of an athlete past his prime and a belly that manages to look both distended and hard, making you think not so much "fat guy" as "strongman," punch more than paunch. His face is flushed though the eyes give you the distinct sense that he has never really felt his hunger to be satisfied. . . . In sum, and to avoid altogether my likely failure at the craft of artistic description, I give you the plain truth: Abu Gamal, even though his name means Progenitor of Beauty, has the conventional features of your generally loathsome person. These are the very same facial features portrayed in old Arabic films, where their mere appearance seems to signal the wickedness of simple souls. Abu Gamal is such a perfect rendering that in spite of everything I can't help but feel some sympathy for him.

Moreover, it appears that the coarseness of Abu Gamal's bodily features imprinted his soul: he acted according to the presumption that he was a thoroughly despicable person hated most energetically by those closest to him. Indeed, he came to terms with these sentiments so perfectly that he even went on to reinforce them with deliberately crude acts and words that he couldn't help, after all, since they were his predestined lot for which he dutifully and constantly praised God. To be truthful about it, and contrary to widespread belief, as tiresome as his coarse behavior is, it was the sole reason why my relationship with him became so firm. After all, crude behavior is one variety of unawareness or unintelligence, the key element of which is, probably, a simple inability to grasp things. So Abu Gamal was basically dense, and I found it painless enough to accept his doings as acts only imaginable coming from a genuinely dim fellow. Dimwit, dope, idiot! Idiots can trash everything we know and we don't get angry about it: we even feel a genuine sense of pity and regret for them.

Even so, he's a person who forces you—the moment you enter his breathing space—to practice a kind of dignity in your dealings with him. So you find yourself transformed into a sort of automaton, though a fervently believing one. You keep your voice at a whisper and consider your words carefully and several times over before you utter them. That's if you say anything in the first place, because his eyes are on the watch for your mistakes, reprimanding you, reminding you constantly of tradition, etiquette, and the irreproachable life. Abu Gamal's face, for all its welts, conveys splendid pride, like the face of a man who is always careful to perform the recognized roles attendant upon right conduct. He offers expansive morning and evening greetings to his neighbors and receives their responses magnanimously; he is never slow to call on the ill or to smile at weddings, and he is sure to locate a front seat inside the tent at other men's funerals.

Abu Gamal went into retirement recently, ending an employment odyssey of thirty-two years in the Helwan Silk Factory. All he retained of it was a proud memory attached to the hand of the great Leader Gamal Abd al-Nasir, which had landed and settled precisely on the nape of his neck, and the irony of his being hired at the age of twenty-two as the very first worker to benefit from the laws on nationalization through which the Leader had consecrated his revolution, followed by his severance and retirement at the age of fifty-four as the first among workers to be let go, owing to the laws of privatization.

Anyway . . . Abu Gamal did not fritter away his time in contemplation of this irony. He adjusted quickly to the whole business of retirement. Indeed, and after some time had passed, naturally, he found it held some advantages over staying on the job. For who knows the unseen? Something grimmer might well have lay in store for him—a person whose talents distinguished him even among those select people who always find opportunity to praise God for everything. Hit by a bicycle, they praise God that it wasn't a car; and if it *was* a car, then—thank the Lord!—it wasn't a train. If one of this select group were to break his arm, he would thank God that his neck was safe, and were he to die—and God forbid *that*!—his family would take up where he left off, praising God that he died a martyr. And so, if such a one is startled to find himself put on pension at an early age, he discovers that this fate came exactly at the right moment for the execution of more important projects.

And so Abu Gamal found it opportune to launch the project he had postponed all along for the sake of raising his four sons. For every one of them—praise God—now lay serene and secure in his wife's embrace inside one of the apartments in the building he had erected for them on the foundations of his own sweating flesh.

The gist of Abu Gamal's scheme lay in the search for some sort of approbation, for respect befitting his head of gray hair. For someone who would give him the eyeball routinely expected by a man of such weight. It seems, though, that Abu Gamal had become thoroughly convinced—through experience, of course—that it was impossible to carry out this project in his own place of residence or in the workplace, or even in the face of any person with whom he had a nodding acquaintance. That he helped out the silk factory's tennis players, and that he insisted on imitating the Chinese by (and only by) riding a bicycle at his age, were enough to rule this out. So he went about searching out his scheme in the faces of strangers.

Abu Gamal always wakes up on schedule, exactly at seven a.m., eats a quick breakfast, and then extracts the hose, his bamboo chair, and the broom he yanked from one of the palm trees at the Helwan silk factory as if in anticipation of this day.

The chair he stations smack in front of the building with a care that lends it the aura of an orator's podium. The hose he shoves onto the mouth of the tap in the building's open stairwell, and the broom he leans against the right half of the double-leaf front door with a lackadaisical manner well suited to tedious work. Next, he takes a little "deducted time" and lights up a cigarette. And then he repeats the whole sequence without a pause but exactly in reverse. Beginning with the broom, he sweeps a strip of street exactly parallel to the front of his building, annexing two additional meters from his neighbors to each side. Next, he takes out the hose to wet down the entire swept expanse, slowly and exactly, after which he adjusts the position of his chair until it is just right and sits down with great self-assurance, Um Gamal's tea always in his right hand (seeing as it's a good thing) and the cigarette in his left hand (seeing as it's a wicked thing) . . . and awaits whatever has been decreed for him. He is ready to pounce on any unfamiliar face, any face as long as he can establish that he has never set eyes on it before. He's got that hunter's sure instinct that his approaching prey will fall. We are on a street, after all, and the streets, as usual, are hardly lacking in strangers.

The moment this face comes in sight, Abu Gamal throws himself into action, his welcoming phrases coming in bursts, surging, supplicating, strenuous, laced with a deeply felt invitation to a glass of tea or even food, and the stranger can find no way out, faced with this hoveringly anxious face and these heartfelt expressions of welcome. The only way out is to comply, to utter the acknowledgment Abu Gamal is searching for, often repeating it several times, sincerely, faithfully, and in unmistakable deference to the addressee. "Thank you, *ya Hagg,* thank you, sir." At which point Abu Gamal goes completely quiet. He is as mute as a man who has just lifted himself off a woman he has desired for a very long time. Or as silent as someone who has obtained a valuable thing that he knows perfectly well he does not deserve.

Finally I reached the corner of our street, and with it the "Neighborhood Salon." As I turned—putting me directly in front of Shaykh Atuwwa's tiny bread bakery—the miraculous truth revealed itself: Abu Gamal's chair was not planted in front of the house, and likewise the strategic zone had not been hosed down ready to receive strangers.

But this wasn't enough to reassure me of the likelihood of sneaking safely all the way to my apartment without some annoying fracas. The absence of a dais does not mean there's no ceremony in progress. Not to mention that it only increases your anxiety if you aren't sure what the next step will bring—and with my very first step over the threshold, the irksome question took me by surprise.

"The stairs are narrow, so how'm I supposed to get by?"

"The stairs are narrow and about to collapse if I'm not careful, and so how am I going to get by you?"

Of course, repeating the question won't solve the problem. Abu Gamal is massive. With his own body, Gamal had squeezed his father into a corner, and they formed an immovable mass right at the point on the staircase that was just broad enough for me to slide by and get away with it unscathed.

"You said, didn't you, you DID say you killed him, you son of a BITCH?"

I could have slunk away, retreated, retraced my steps to find some café where I could waste a little time until Gamal would have finished pummeling his father for lying. (Sayf had returned in one piece, after Abu Gamal had claimed he'd sucked the kid's blood dry, off in some empty trash lot). But the novelistic character I've chosen for myself ruled out such a possibility. How could my character take cover now, and in this cowardly manner, and withdraw from such significant events, especially when the two parties to this quarrel held the position of Gamal and his father?

Until recently I believed that a person's life unfolds along a line that shoots straight away from his past. The farther time carries you, I thought, the surer you can be that this past will not repeat itself. I even had an image in my mind's eye that illustrates my conviction perfectly. "The present," as we call it, is a train we've boarded. Our pasts are made up of scenes and personalities that drop from view the moment our train rushes by, abandoning them to each side. From our perspectives, as we sit in that train, everything seems to pass so quickly. The past is for *back there*, for forgetting; and the present is given to the past, which swallows it. Our life's meaning is its end, marked out from the start. But the repetition of the fights in this house has made me doubt all of that. Indeed, those fights have convinced me from up close that the past may well return. I can see now that anyone's life is nothing but an assemblage of repeated scenes.

When I first moved in, I would rush into those fights unthinkingly, exactly like a son of the village and every bit as naïve as a country yokel, shouting, *"Ayb ya gamaa'a!* For shame! Is this any way to behave?" Because of the age factor, I would always look to Abu Gamal first, and then I would whirl around to face Gamal, sending the blame his way with the usual phrases about fatherhood and the duties of sons, although I was sure that he didn't respect a single word I said. In fact, the fight would end with an impressive number of words flung at my face from both sides. I accepted it all with a graciousness that I considered an occasion for pride, comparing myself to the venerable head of a tribe who has to endure the rage of both adversaries in order to make peace between them.

Now, though, I was afraid, as I paused at the landing halfway up the staircase to watch and wait. I still had a way to go: my apartment was two floors above. Gamal was fully occupied in applying his knife to his father's neck. I estimated each leg of the distance I'd have to go, with a precision acquired from my skill at dashing across streets directly in front of speeding vehicles. I even took into account the extra space I needed if I were to avoid a collision between my face and a fist that might chance to stray from its usual course. I waited for just the right moment, and when Gamal yanked his father close I sped by them with an elegance I mulled over a few minutes later, after I was inside my apartment and breathing easier. It had been an embarrassingly tight fit, with my nose and Abu Gamal's tremendous back sharing the same narrow space on the stairs, so tight that I figured the reason his back was quivering was that my breaths were jetting out quick and hard. Gamal's back had been against the railing, and it was my good luck that he was completely absorbed in the matter at hand. No sooner had I squeezed by behind Abu Gamal's back—with an ordinary, casual hello such as I always offer when they're eating or watching a football match—than they ended the quarrel suddenly to stare after me. . . . Why, I don't know. Were they admiring what I'd just performed as a character from a novel, or were they irritated by what I'd done in my capacity as a new resident in the family building?

Abu Gamal is a decent man, and so is Gamal, and I'm a decent man, too. People are basically decent. But something is simply and fundamentally out of whack here. The two of them are passionate about their daily argument, which never goes beyond swearing, spitting, and waving weapons in the air. The underlying and covert reason for it is a struggle for authority when it comes to the family building. The public rationale is a difference of opinion over how best to treat Sayf's insane behavior, which has dragged the family's honorable reputation into the mud. It's an everyday quarrel that doesn't sever the bonds of affection but in fact, perhaps, strengthens them. That seems to be the case, anyway, because after it's over they discover that *we only got each other, and nothing lasts for nobody.* Meanwhile, someone has been putting food on the table for the two of them. And anyway, what's wrong with whetting an appetite with a few verbal slings, the devil and anger and insanity? God's curses on Sayf and the day he was born.

As for me, I'm all in favor of a different quarrel, a bloody fight that brings on a permanent hostility through which I can guarantee my security and my release from a haunting and persistent fear that they'll unite against me—an instinctive phobia that lay behind my flight from the Bedouin hamlets to Cairo, only to find, here, that it's the sole guarantee of my safety among these people.

2

In some shape or form, we all carry in our depths a pathetic actor who plays one role over the course of a lifetime, a role restricted by circumstances of work and family, by propriety and traditions and our always unsparing consciences. If we are going to perform our roles well, we must live as masked figures and we must never cease suppressing our true desires. Our audience—which we draw not only from the people closest to us but also from ourselves (inside us are the actor and the spectator both)—is a fierce and demanding one, ready to pounce on anything unexpected. If a middle-aged man rebels against acting his part—one of dignity and wisdom—and instead takes on the role of an adolescent for a while, we sneer at him. If our children take up arms against wide-eyed gullibility in favor of playing it wicked for a spell, we're instantly suspicious of their motives. And so when a young man's talents steer him toward the role of a young woman, we torment him and label him in all sorts of ways, the least burdensome of which is "insane."

Sayf was not insane. He wasn't mad, nor was he narrow or shortsighted, seeing his own affairs through a single lens and dividing everything into two categories: for him or against him. He was simply a rebellious actor and a giddy lover.

He was an actor in revolt against limiting his life to the performance of a single role (because he believed life held room for more), and a lover devoted to a renown he felt he deserved.

Sayf perfected the role of poet and had dreams of attaining the prestige and distinction of a famous versifier, but when he realized early on that a singer attracts far more prestige and fame than does a poet, he devoted himself to song. And he did actually sing for several weddings in our street, which enabled him (and this was their only plus) to try out a different role that suited him well—the role of ladies' coiffeur, which drove singing out of his mind completely. That's because he didn't stop at playing this role faithfully but rather went on to fall passionately in love with his customers. His love was so sincere that he decided it would be sensible to start looking as much like them as he could.

Last of the brood for Abu Gamal, Sayf isn't like other eighteen-year-olds. No impulsiveness there, no spontaneity, no adolescent immaturity. His gaze puts me in mind of a meek lamb on the cusp of a future as a destructive, predatory wolf. He's fairly slim, with features not out of the ordinary—just features—and there's nothing in particular to draw one's attention. Yet if he walks by, you simply can't avoid staring hard at him. Perhaps that is why he makes a point of walking extremely slowly, as if he's aware that people are looking at him and he wants to give them a chance to get in a really good look.

Whatever Sayf has wanted to do he has done—except for fulfilling one simple longing: to enjoy an evening promenade wearing a miniskirt he bought at the Tahrir Center Mall, a sleeveless bodysuit, and a wig he kept that used to belong to the hair salon. Sad to say, though, his brothers' fierceness, especially Gamal's, has kept him from making it happen.

Sayf has a passion for fishing around in subjects that make others blush, but he always drops a heavy curtain over these topics—which makes you want to shield him from embarrassment and convinces you in a practical way that there is nothing really illicit going on. I was sure of this even after he came over very late one night to play that cassette hot with the *aahs* he and his buddies had recorded together. He didn't call it what it deserved, didn't use the common name for this sort of recording. He said it was just an evening gathering he described as "wholesome," an evening bringing together friends who were even more wholesome. And he didn't *do* anything, even though I'm sure he picked up signals that I was amenable to that sort of evening. He just gave me the type of look that has come to be described as "deep." This really did throw me into confusion, not out of embarrassment but because I didn't know, from this look of his, what exactly was expected of me, especially since, to be honest, I had completely failed to single out his voice in the *aahaat* tape.

All he did was to stand up and turn around slowly. When he calculated that his behind was hanging level with the top of my shoulder, he rubbed his backside against me lightly, again and again, slight and recurring touches, like those of a skillfully handled paintbrush against a wall that's been finely sandpapered. Touches you couldn't exactly condemn (if you were to count yourself among the godly), but not ones you could applaud, either (if you are part of that rare group with something to say on such issues). Touches that put you squarely in no-man's-land, and wondering which way to go; that saddle you with a troublesome indecisiveness you can't resolve.

If I react and throw him out there's always the possibility that I didn't understand his noble intentions. But if I shower him with kisses

*and touches, it's possible that he'll do it, too, and then who knows, it might
turn into a major scandal that will bring to a fast and nasty end all the efforts I've made to build my good name.*

Since coming to live in this part of town, I have maintained a
blameless life (after a fashion) and a kindhearted appearance, and
probably also I've convinced people that I'm abstemious and a bit
stupid. I rely on all of this to deal with my fear of my neighbors at
this address. A person with carefully cultivated idiocy makes
everyone around him feel secure. More important, everyone will
work hard to keep the idiot outside the circle of their conflicts.

Fear is the surest refuge for anyone in circumstances like
mine. It is natural to feel afraid when one finds oneself at the top
of a sheer and rocky cliff or when one has to confront a mass of
strangers. Fear and a good name, they're the key. When you have
no choice but to settle in a strange place among people whose
wickedness you know you won't be able to withstand for long,
you've got to seek out a good reputation. An unblemished name,
plus shrinking your longings a bit. The better a person keeps
himself in check, the closer he gets to the hearts of others. . . .

For the soul doth enjoin unto evil, says the Qur'an.[1]

It isn't really quite this bleak, but everyone does have their
own legitimate driving ambitions. Okay, let's ditch "driving ambitions," which has a ring of accusation to it. Let's just say that
everyone has legitimate aspirations. As honorable as they are,
though, one's aspirations always get in the way of other people's
desires, which are no less creditable than one's own. Here's
where hate crops up. As much as I'm able, I try to curb my aspirations, not because I want people to be fond of me—I have

1. Qur'an 12.53.

great respect for hate—but because my desire to realize swift and humiliating victories for my enemies makes the average interaction with hate more powerful than the joy of victory itself. So much so that, in flight from the flames of that desire, I rush headlong to give myself up on the spot to my enemies, even though, when it comes to slight and recurring touches, I freeze with confusion and indecision.

Sayf always leaves the door ajar and reserves the right to open or close it. He's intent on penciling his eyebrows and is especially skilled at highlighting his every feature with face powder, giving a greater share of attention to his lips, for which he reserves a coffee-brown color appropriate to the warm tones of his complexion. He tirelessly admires his own manly sexual prowess, and his trousers—he wears a variety of brand names—fit that much more tightly because his behind puffs out.

And then. . . .

And then . . . he lit the fire. On himself. He went and bought a jerry can of cooking fuel from Hasan the grocer and with his own hands he distributed it across the folds of his body, taking care that the gas reached all its slopes, especially his backside, to which he allotted a whole handful and rubbed as hard as the most zealous believer performing his ablutions. (This severe rubbing we must not take too seriously. We mustn't attribute meaning to it. It's just an especially stern version of the yearning for exactness and precision you'd find in any alert conscience that is in sync with its possessor, who will face God Himself after a finite number of seconds.) And then Sayf pulled out the box of matches, slowly. . . . And from that day on, he found this business so pleasant that he would regularly buy a can of kerosene from Hasan the grocer.

I wonder, though, why he always chose this strident way to flee toward death. Was he looking for a celebrity status that would be worthy of Sayf Son of Abu Gamal? Or for a new role that no one but he was strong enough to play? Or was it the cruelty of fear, which transforms death into a bearable existence?

Death is one of the options you always have before you as a simple means of eliminating whatever danger it is that you face. Death is the endpoint of every danger, and at the same time it's the exemplary way to make your peace with all those dangers out there. It's far more calming, for instance, to be flattened by a car, or by a stray bullet or a strong narcotic, than to be quaking on your feet before some particular peril. Perhaps if he had actually died Sayf would have saved his own self from being forgotten and lost, just as the glowing coal saves the Bedouin from losing his way in the desert. Perhaps then I would have told his story in a manner to evoke the awe and praise dead people ordinarily have the good fortune to enjoy. (I've failed to find a clear reason for this respectful reaction. After all, death is as easy as leaving a person you're sure you'll never see again.) It isn't even far-fetched to imagine Sayf's name suspended above the salon at the corner of our street, and there's no doubt that the people in our building would have shown they were proud that he lived among them, as is the case with my father, whom I never saw. My mother always summed him up with one perfectly apt expression: "He pulled his hand away from all good yields to set it down firmly on barren fields." Despite that, and even though he didn't have Sayf's courage about lighting fires but rather died a banal, possibly even shameful, death as a natural outcome of his addiction to a certain kind of adulterated hash, my father's story always wafted from the tongues of our tribe's sons perfumed with words of eulogy and respect. You might even call it sainthood, to the point where my mother sometimes forgot that business about his hand and the barren fields, and her facial muscles would go soft as she said, gruffly, "He was a good man!"

The tragedy of my father's life, which he never found a way to resolve, lay in his occupation as a government watchman, a line of work in which Bedouin offspring specialized after leaving the desert for good to settle on the fringes of cities and towns. The job was exclusively theirs for one single reason: the courage for which they were so famous.

There's a particular kind of boldness that arises from the nomadic life of the deserts. If you are moving on from a certain place, then you are the strongest one in it and everyone else is a little afraid of you. They're in awe because here you are, going away tomorrow, and to go away is tantamount to dying, at least as far as the people of that place are concerned. It's easy to conclude from this that the person who is leaving must feel no fear about anything, and it is just as natural to find everyone praising his courage to the skies. This clear-cut kind of fear, one that has a known, specific object, is unsuitable to nomads. They devote themselves to a different sort of fear, a hard-to-define fear in whose authority they profoundly believe.

They are certainly believers. They are instinctual believers. Life in the desert is always threatened by murky, ambiguous things. They're things as unclear and uncertain and ominous as the vanishing mouth of a well, the absent rain, getting lost, the severity of a viper's bite. Faced with experiences like these, one has to fortify oneself with belief in other things, things that are no less doubtful or obscured, which the Bedouin call *qadar,* fate, or *namus,* the natural law of things and of honor, or the curse of the ancestors.

But that is a different subject. Let's return to my father who despised and felt demeaned by his line of work. He considered the life of a merchant more fitting to his ancestry and dignity.

I don't know why he chose that profession over any other. He could have aimed to become an airplane pilot or a soccer player or an actor. Any of these would have worked fine, since the issue remained simply a question of aspirations, hardly likely to become reality anyway.

All his life my father was preparing himself for the business of commerce. It was for the sake of commerce that he was never actually at the school that he had been assigned to patrol. He took advantage of the sleazy nature of the corporal responsible for monitoring watchmen's absences. But when the head officer discovered that my father wasn't showing up for work, he summoned my father, not only to punish him but also to hunt for some clear and explicable reason for his arrogance. "If you're absent again, you're walking," he warned him. "I'll put you on trial." With a confidence that confirmed his natural superiority, my father rebutted the threat with a muttered Bedouin proverb. "Lighter than a dry camel turd on a windy day. We want to stay away, we will. Write me down in that book 'absent,' we'll just rub it out. Another ten pennies for Mr. Officer there with his absences."

It was an event to remember. The bribed corporal had to resign. The investigator gave my father only a month in the pen because he took my father's words to the officers for a confession of the crime.

My father came out of jail full of determination to go into his chosen profession, commerce. He opened the first grocery our tiny southern Egyptian settlement of Bedouin had ever had. He filled the shelves with every variety of food and all the sweets he was fond of himself, relying on the assumption that if he loved it, so would the customers. Naturally, the business failed. Not because his assumption was wrong, but because every time a customer requested a certain thing from our shop my father would remember immediately that *he* loved and craved it. All of the merchandise went untouched to our home.

My father wasn't badly upset by the failure. As he always said, "Commerce is a gamble. Might lead to profit, might lead to loss—that's the secret of its beauty." My father always had a supply of platitudes at hand to justify his fantasies. He failed in the grocery venture, so let him try his luck at another idea.

And this other project required—to break the hold of bad luck—a trip.

"A trip! Where to?"

"Ismailiyya."

My father sold his land, and with my mother in tow he headed for Ismailiyya.

"Why?"

"Buying and selling."

"What gets bought and sold in Ismailiyya?" I don't know. But I do know very well that he and my mother went back to the settlement. My parents returned there two months later by two different routes. He came by the police-station route. She sat in the railway station crying until someone very kind came along and stayed by her side as far as the outskirts of the settlement.

The police-station route was pretty harsh, it seems, because my father decided to stay permanently and categorically in the village. He returned to his old work as a civil-service watchman and picked up where he'd left off with his commercial aspirations. But he did so in an entirely different form that protected

him from the risk. Now he advised others on commercial enter-
prises that were sure to profit. It turned out that every project on
which he consulted was enormously successful. He became the
Mecca for anyone who was aspiring to enter the commercial
world.

So it seems that my father really *was* a merchant. A skilled
and clever one, in fact, whose role consisted exclusively of
dreaming up successful ventures. But when it came to imple-
menting and managing them, he was absolutely the wrong guy.

3

A vehicle stopped in front of No. 36. As people often do in such situations, my wife contorted her face into an expression of deep concern that failed to mask her delight, so that her face looked comical as she said, "It's the paddy wagon."

Sayf climbed in with a cool poise that revealed how vast is the imagination of the directors of Arabic films in which madness strikes down one of the heroes, since in this case there was absolutely no indication of the white jacket that usually provokes the hero, as if it's the whiteness of the coats that lets them know they're crazy. At this point emerges the sole importance of this pair of boors who tie up the disturbed hero in a frequently rerun scene from one of those 1950s tearjerkers directed by Hasan al-Imam.

Sayf came out the front door wearing one of his carefully coordinated outfits. He greeted the driver and his sidekicks as if they were pals, stuck out his tongue in the direction of his brother Gamal, spit in his father's face, and swore on his mother's religion, his voice growing appropriately louder in view of her location. She was watching from the third-floor balcony next to mine. Then Sayf looked right at me. It occurred to me suddenly that I could part permanently with the twenty pounds he had borrowed from me after all. He shifted his gaze immediately, and the car shot off. I expressed my sympathy for him in silence by imagining the scene: Sayf in the loony bin, just like I've seen it in films.

Since I really *am* very sympathetic to him, the scene appeared in full, with all of the details. Sayf in blinding white clothes. His hair would have to be all tousled, as he stood amidst a gang of crazies, and one of them would emerge having taken on the features of the interrogators. No doubt he really did go nuts during one of the interrogations.

"Name."

"Sayf."

So he writes down the name slowly, meticulously, in a register that lies open in front of him. He speaks. "Sayf means sword. What is your *name?*"

But the rest of the dialogue is lost in the racket coming from the television, since as usual my wife has turned up the volume.

It's Gamal who worked tirelessly for this—for the sake of dumping Sayf in the loony bin. It's true that all the residents of our building, my wife included, would chat openly about how crazy Sayf was. But Gamal was the only one who relayed the news to the proper authorities, the ones with the insanity portfolio. Then Gamal worked his numerous connections to high-level bureaucrats, trying to hasten Sayf's entry into the hospital by getting around the required medical examination.

It was Gamal, then, who showed how happy he was about Sayf's disappearance by hosting an evening of *bango* that went on until morning. My share was three whole joints of really fine pot, which put a definitive end to my quarrel with him. I had no problem acknowledging in return how naïve was the sympathy I had felt for Sayf, which I expressed by imagining a scenario that didn't actually take place, one involving the mental hospital.

Abd al-Halim, man of the house, father of the children, was around when this happened. Sayf's getting into the van stirred him up, but it was a weak excuse for an outburst, nothing more than roundly cursing Gamal—but not because he was torn up about Sayf, whom after all he had tried to kill so that the household could rest easier. Abd al-Halim was mad because it was Gamal who had put Sayf in the hospital, which he considered blatant interference in matters that were his own to decide. Wasn't he the elder of the building, the one whose word was law? Then, how could it not have been *him* who informed the authorities of his son's insanity? It was a scandal. How could he look folks in the eye ever again?

Gamal and Abd al-Halim were in agreement on one thing. Sayf had to be gotten rid of. They even had the same rationale, which was that Sayf had dragged the family's good name through the mud and all of Manshiyat Nasir knew that he was a limp wrist. Or, more accurately, a bottom.

Abd al-Halim had failed to get rid of Sayf by luring him to one of the empty lots nearby in order to kill him. Gamal, on the other hand, had actually brought his scheme to fruition, disposing of Sayf inside the walls of the insane asylum. Not because he was more merciful than his father, nor because he worried about somehow confirming suspicions around his narcotics business. He had no fear at all where that was concerned. When Sayf threatened him during one argument by declaring he would inform on his brother, Gamal just said—with a self-assurance you'd expect from a guy like him—"#!*@ your mother!" Gamal did what he did because getting rid of Sayf by killing him would "make the pimp's words law over the whole place." That's what he couldn't possibly allow to happen.

🏵 Gamal is the eldest of Abd al-Halim's sons, and that is why he is so self-confident that he can sum up his own father in a single and highly functional sentence: "Man's a pimp." A sentence that when it's uttered—and I don't know why this is—gets Abd al-Halim's gaze dropping immediately to the ground. Is this an admission that he admires the neat brevity in the sentence's construction, or does it get right to the heart of something so close to home that he's incapable of reacting in any other manner?

Gamal's moniker means "Gorgeousness," but I really should call him the Guy with Style. He is one of those people who seem most at ease when you call them by their first names even though you have just met them. Gamal is the sort of person in whose company you can relive your childhood, all your silliness. You can recall your rash behavior and all those stupid things you used to do. Maybe, even, in front of such people, you bring up the subject of your own simpleminded tendencies, and you refer to these with total ease, without worrying that their eyes are studying you, that they're lying in wait to rebuke you and remind you emphatically of traditions and suitability and good comportment and best behavior. From the first glance you have no doubt at all that a guy such as Gamal is a genuine offshoot of one of those families of pedigree . . . pedigree and absurd, repugnant wealth.

A youth who has just hit forty and always wears the latest fashions as he sits smugly behind the wheel of the latest-model car, swinging it through one of the city's wild-growing, unplanned zones—that's Gamal. Sits behind that wheel and on top of a deeply embedded heritage of renown that has grown deeper across four liaisons that are now known as far as the residential fringes of Helwan and al-Maasara, and the sparks of which have traveled by microbus right to the heart of Cairo. These are relationships he managed with a panache and technique that one has to appreciate. He has one technique which he always uses, and that's all . . . an unexpected approach, but it's apt considering his desire to challenge something for the sake of the challenge. Something vaguely defined that caused him to disdain pleasures of the body that were easily gotten and safe, that he could acquire effortlessly in the arms of a God-given, allowable woman such as his wife, far from prying eyes and scandal. An unexplained urge that compelled him to struggle for the sake of a different delight, a pleasure tinged with apprehension, the joy of the hunt; pleasure snatched out of the lion's mouth and in spite of the merciless eyes of people. A rare pleasure that he could find only with women of chastity—those ladies who are so very "well protected" in their homes and by their honor.

When one of these *masunat* attracts him, Gamal simply ignores this well-protected's husband and anyone else she associates with, making straight for her with no deviousness, armed not so much with his oppressive elegance as with his skill at storytelling. Gamal is a real storyteller, and his tales have a stunning magic whose power only women know.

His first relationship followed immediately upon marriage (her marriage to his neighbor, and his marriage to Hanan, his cousin through his mother). The woman was good-looking. Good-looking and alluring in the way of a woman Naguib Mahfouz described some time ago in his novel *The Riffraff*—this woman looked pretty much like that character. She was the daughter of neighbors, and I don't know why she held no appeal for Gamal before her wedding night.

What did it was a routine visit to the neighbors to offer the usual congratulations and wishes for a happy marriage. At the very moment in which they were offering the usual marriage sweets to the rhythm of a smile-infested and fortifying conversation with the bride and groom, an incident took place that Gamal hadn't expected in the slightest. Because speech in such social visits normally is confined to tedious compliments that everyone knows by heart, he let his imagination loose, and there he found a resource to draw on in the monotony of the visit. He imagined a scene: the bride appears stark naked and completely bewildered, and the groom has thrown himself at her feet, putting his head in his hands . . . a scene with a meaning that doesn't need much explanation. To lighten the severity of this scene Gamal reran it, but he made a minor adjustment. This time the groom had vanished, to resume his weeping elsewhere. The bride was still there, as naked as before, but with a different man, who was attempting to soothe her. Before this man's features could come into focus in Gamal's head, he came to and realized how strongly he was pressing on the groom's hand as he said "good-bye" and "thank you" at the apartment's front door.

In Gamal's coming visits, the image in his head would turn into reality. And the features of the man in the scene would grow sharper, revealing the outlines of Gamal's body, and Gamal would not stop, naturally, with soothing her. Here emerges the dramatic core of the repeated story whose chapters were transmitted quickly to all remaining residents of Manshiyat Nasir. The groom had caught his bride with Gamal four times, her sister twice, and her mother once (only once, because she was just visiting), and all of them confirmed the scene without showing any evidence of embarrassment or any apparent desire to make accusations, as if this relationship was a sort of fate that one simply had to give in to, praising God all the while for His Doings. Even the groom justified his insistence on moving away from Manshiya with a detailed narrative exclusively concerning "the wife," as if he were not talking about a certain man whom he had spotted directly on top of her.

🙦 Gamal began his working life by pushing drugs. In fact, though, he had no prior plans to enter this sector, since he lacked the talents characteristic of its captains of commerce. It was merely a coincidence that he was bent on exploiting. He was your typical coddled youth, the teenaged leader of the gang who doesn't rest until all the guys are coming over to his place of an evening. They could find all means of entertainment here, after all: dominoes, backgammon, chess, videos and music cassettes, and topnotch ingredients on the hookah, all in all a first-class space with plenty of room to spread out in and no fears of discovery. That was because there was no strict father averse to the follies of youth hovering nearby, no patriarch whom they could expect to crash the evening at any moment as most fathers do. It wasn't that Gamal's papa was away. In fact, he was very much there, all smiles and liberal-handed, so over-the-top that he even waited on them, selecting the latest tunes, tamping down the bowl of the water pipe and lighting it. Well, they were his first-born son's pals, weren't they? "Why, if the earth didn't keep them afloat, he'd carry them himself, on his own head if he had to."

No throne comes without its costs. Every night, those good friends fell upon the bowl and it was gone with a single inhalation, leaving the boss frantically searching out a new source where he could secure a new chunk well in advance of the next convivial evening, which was always looming. To extract himself from this daily predicament the leader considered mounting a corrective revolution pertaining to these nightly get-togethers, a socialist revolution that would compel everyone to have a part in crafting the resolution on hashish under his leadership. He would assume direct command of purchasing, due to considerations of leadership, procuring a goodly lump from his uncle and father-in-law, Abu Hanan. He would carve it into equal portions, one for each member of the clique, and at the end of the evening soirée accounts would be reckoned. From each member Gamal would receive—in cash—the equivalent of whatever he had consumed in the course of the evening.

The revolution was such a stunning success that the business was launched without delay. The boss put cash on the line . . . a chunk worth a thousand pounds . . . from the scales (very sensitive) each member of the clique took his share . . . the wheel of commerce turned, the lump became two lumps, three, ten. The scales worked overtime; the hashheads reeled and bid and outdid one another, as the numbers mounted and the boss counted, and the debts piling up in his head fed his cheer. For he was leader and captain and as high as he'd ever been, and the sum swelled inside his head, because he had been thinking exclusively about the sum required from the group, and he hadn't thought at all about the sum required from him for the debts he'd incurred to get those successive chunks of hash. Waking up to that fact forced him to acknowledge that his revolution was a flop. The liberality of the guys in the neighborhood, as is typical when it comes to friends, went only as far as their insistence on knowing what the bill for the hash would amount to, *before* the evening session got under way. Later, after all the smoking and all the fun, at the end of the night, they quietly withdrew, one after another, from the leader's field of vision without paying what they owed.

"Hey man, don't stress, I mean, where are we gonna go anyway, man?"

The upshot was that Gamal found out he was under the gun for ten grand, owed to his in-law the trafficker, who threatened him openly with murder. "This stuff isn't child's play and there's no 'c'mon go easy on me' in it." In the midst of his cogitations as he tried to find a way out of this mess Gamal wrote:

We are men of minds
Minds enough to uncover missteps
Whatever the blunder
Regretfully though
Regretful so
Our intelligence is slow:
Slow.

So slow we uncover our missteps after we've stumbled and fallen, and naturally, then, our discoveries have the look of futility.

Gamal is a writer. A writer who produces little, remains obscure, and detests having people read his creative output. Or, more precisely, he is a thinker who occasionally gives in to a desire to put his thoughts into writing. Not to address a particular reader, however. He has no respect for such a disposition, and believes that his writing is a sacrosanct and precious thing that ought not to be shared with anyone. He sees it as a personal belonging exactly in the way his funds are his to dispense with. Gamal writes, therefore, solely for the purpose of rendering his knowledge of life as precisely as he can, of working on it. He writes in order to defend his personal philosophy before his conscience, which offers no mercy and has no time for those writers who so undervalue their thoughts and their inscriptions that they scatter them profusely and broadcast them everywhere. Thoughts are like money and real estate: it would be insanity to hand them out freely to whoever happens to be passing by.

Gamal has confidence in himself and is prepared to make an immediate sacrifice of anything he suspects might affect his ease of mind adversely, even if it is his own children. This puts him at risk of appearing arrogant as he fulfills his destiny as writer; or, rather, as he defends his take on things: "Some may be preoccupied with improving the world, but all that occupies me is my own little self. I rock it gently, and I regularly give it a lot of close attention. And on occasion I see myself as the grandest man in the world . . . just for a fleeting moment and soon enough it disappears, but those around me—always—are blessed with just enough alertness to seize that moment, and words go around about my self-regard . . . while at another moment—which comes up just as suddenly and unexpectedly—I feel I am very weak, weaker than a mosquito, and scared even of my own clothes, but sadly—so sadly—at that moment no one sees me, no one gives me a reassuring pat on the shoulder."

It's a question of the self. And of interests particular to that self. No more, no less. He writes: "The murderer friend of *Shaykh* Zossima in *The Brothers Karamazov* committed a grievous error when he made personal interest responsible for the world's mistakes. It seems that the nature of the era in which Dostoevsky lived blinded this man to seeing life as a wise man such as he was would normally view it. A person's acts emerge from his self, from his individuality, from those very limited personal interests that go no further than food, clothing, and hash-stuffed fags. The more personal a deed is in its nature, the more sincere it is. How genuine the hungry man is when he thinks of food, how earnest the filthy body when it longs for a cake of perfumed soap, and how sweet the delight of the addict when he succeeds in concocting a new and powerful blend that protects him from a troubling warren of thought that leads him to ponder the likelihood that the world's known narcotics are sparse indeed."

4

"He bestows upon you your livelihood as He so grants it to the birds: *khumasan,* you are fed, and *bitatan,* you reemerge."[1] So said "Prof" Ramadan with an assured flourish of eloquence (and this was utterly in character). He said this in response to Abu Gamal's story. Or in response to his complaint.

Even though I had only a foggy sense of the meaning of these unfamiliar words *khumasan* and *bitatan,* I was satisfied to leave it at that, guessing that they had something to do with divine generosity. But Abu Gamal—because his hand was in the flames—wasn't content with guesswork, and furthermore, he took it as an insinuation from the professor that Abu Gamal's exertions were coming to zilch. So his response was sharp. "Meaning what, Prof? *Khumasan* and *bitatan* and shit. What is all of this crap, anyway?—*Empty-bellied you are fed, rotund you reemerge . . .*" He rose, literally, to the attack: "What *exactly* is your point?"

We were sitting in front of the house. Abu Gamal had just finished readying the place for his daily assembly. He was exhausted from overwork, and, to be perfectly honest about it, his

---

1. From the *Hadith,* or reported acts and sayings of the Prophet Muhammad, a signal source of practice for Muslims.

anger was both dignified and justified. He had not expected a lecture in jurisprudence that would attribute his toil to God, giving short shrift to his own daily tribulations. To the contrary, he longed hungrily for a simple word of praise, nothing on paper, no more than a word or two out loud to express some consideration for his self-sacrifices—and if only we would show a little dismay over his situation, the lot of good, well-meaning, hardworking fathers faced with the foolishness of rebellious sons!

To get to the point, Abu Gamal told me and the Prof a story that concerned him (and only him). This was the saga of daily meals and immoderate numbers of cigarettes: "It's too early in the morning, but there I am anyway running off to the souk. I bring bread hot from the bakery, *ful* beans and *taamiya* and greens and the rest, and I come in, well, I find Um Gamal, she's already done up the platters, every apartment a plate, we divide out the food, same thing *exactly* onto every platter, and then, later morning, God love you, signs of their presence start to show, wife of every last one of those blasted louts puts in an appearance, sashaying here and there and hanging around to get her hands on everything she can from those louts' father while the blasted boys are still between the sheets no cares in the world. Amer and his woman a plate. Salah and Nahid, that's two. Even Sayf (and may Allah return him from the madhouse), his mama makes him a platter, every last thing on it, and sits there crying over it, and begs our Lord to release him, and then the damn cigs, pack after pack I'm handing out, and I find that every one of those boys he's inhaling a pack every couple hours then creeping back to me all daddy's boy with his head hanging at his nuts wanting another pack. So it gets to the point where I'm buying one pack splitting it up and sending each one of 'em five fags and the boy finishes 'em off and is back in my face, so am I gonna keep up with this every damn day? And your fine fellow Gamal Mr. Efficient, who swipes from the lawyer a little and then a little more, when it comes to his pop his ears are stuffed with dirt and dough. And it's 'bring on the bango, bring on some broads,' and I'm like you know I don't have more'na damn penny or two in my pension, and then you say to me 'Our Lord . . .'—Lord what, Prof!— bless the Prophet and GIVE ME A BREAK."

Ustadh Ramadan lives on the second floor just beneath my apartment and facing Amer's, and he's always defending Amer in the onslaught of Abu Gamal's endless attacks, not out of loyalty to the sanctity of neighbors as much as for the sake of the eyes of Amer's wife Zannuba.

At nine o'clock every night he presses the bell at his neighbors' door. Zannuba opens the door with a jolt that at least looks like eagerness. "Allah! My goodness, why it's the Ustadh!" She makes as if to shut the door in his face but without any noticeable delay she reopens it, slowly this time to allow an admiring look to creep across the doorway, parceled up with a cunning smile that heralds a promise he's certain won't ever come to fulfillment. "Please, come on in, Amer's home, he's in there," and he steps across the threshold with such extreme politeness that his bearing is one of abject contrition, and while she steeps the cinnamon that he's bought for them out of his own pocket, he kills some time with Amer exchanging small talk.

"Welcome, welcome, you honor us."

"May God honor your capabilities."

"How're you doing?"

"Praise be to God!"

"Lord, now, I've missed you."

"God preserve and keep you."

"And the school."

"Fine, fine."

An exchange that neither one hears despite the warmth of their tones, since its only importance lies in charging the atmosphere properly for the moment of farewell that all of them anticipate. The Prof drinks his hot cinnamon quickly because there is always some important matter awaiting him, and he leaves the same way he came in, his face to the ground like the polite and self-respecting gentleman that he is. As he cracks open the door to his own apartment, the game comes to its close: his ears suck in Zannuba's parting incantation. "Have a good night, Ustadh." Later he enjoys a deep and healthful sleep.

Amer has the Prof's number on this one. He approves of this entertainment and warms up the ambiance for him. For the sake of his pastime, the Prof willingly assumes payment for the little packet of bango that Amer smokes daily, not to mention that Amer—and here's what's most important—has no anxieties about the Prof's gifts when it comes to the women.

The Prof teaches Arabic at the Helwan Experimental School. The first thing he'll say upon meeting you is that his wife hails from Beni Sweif. *The Beauty Queen of Beni Sweif,* that's what he says. When you show your astonishment—as he anticipates you will, especially if you know her personally—he launches into the history that he so loves. Or, to put it more accurately, that he lives in. When a guy finds nothing compelling in his life, and when he knows for certain that a moment's passing has meaning only in that it hastens his destined end, he has to esteem history and delve into the past. Into the moments that really did happen, for that's the one thing he truly possesses.

The Prof will declare with a confidence befitting the wise that in the corrupt age of the royalists competitive beauty pageants were held in every governorate in the country. He'll launch into a very full description of the particulars of those competitions and their protocol, and he'll recount a long list of the women who emerged as winners on the national level—all those beauty queens of the republic. And because he's expecting that it might irritate you to hear him jumbling up the monarchical period with the republican era, he'll advise you earnestly not to worry your brain over these insignificant matters, going on to explain—with evidence and proofs—that it really doesn't make much difference. In the meantime, he's either overlooking or staying far away from the plain fact that your irritation comes from a different source, a material one with no connection to history or politics, which is the serious slide in the level of beauty in Beni Sweif. The Prof's wife richly deserves Sancho Panza's description of the Bold Knight's beloved in *Don Quixote*. Though she's constantly engrossed in an exhausting self-beautification campaign, all it ever amounts to is a head-turning, off-putting mess, bits of Western and Eastern and African clothing entangling a body so emaciated it's most likely to remind you of a rat on the prowl.

Prof Ramadan is coming up on sixty. To his own mind, he's a study in venerability and measured action, exuding these signs of wisdom that he regards as his rightful adornments.

Unlike me, the Ustadh didn't move into No. 36 as an inexperienced newlywed. No, the Prof arrived here having already attained his ebb stage, an age of ennui and insight. He had been living in his dad's lavish building in Hadayiq al-Qubba, the upmarket Gardens of the Cupola. But his wife's unending problems with his brothers and sisters—who also lived in the building—denied him the opportunity to ponder life's circumstances with any depth. He had no choice but to leave his father's building behind and with it the entire district. He made his mind up to reside at the very edge of Cairo since there he would find calm and an atmosphere perfect for the contemplative life. Manshiyat Gamal Abd al-Nasir, therefore, suited his needs perfectly.

He keeps his thinking equipment in good condition. To be more precise, all his acts and paraphernalia are related in some way to this concern of his: the dense spectacles, black-framed and hanging on a silver chain; the pipe successfully purchased, after strenuous effort, from one of the nations of Latin America following upon his admiration for a legend retold in *The Gift*; the antique watch that spurred him to believe that time carries value; and finally, the inkwell and peacock feather with which he inscribes his poetry.

For Ramadan is a poet and raconteur of fecund imagination. He always buttresses his own turns of phrase with supporting sentences and aphorisms from the high tradition to lend a whiff of dignity to his accounts—especially those concerning sex, which can be an important source of inspiration. Take me for an example. Before I was so fortunate as to hear the affecting (and blistering) details of those tales, I found it extremely difficult to compose my own story with any female so I could tell it to myself while I plied the secret act. Thanks to these narratives, too, I spared my brain the wear and tear of having to imagine real-life events whose heroine was always his wife.

At first the Prof related his marital adventures to me with a shy reticence. His bashfulness cast his stories in a cryptic form. As our relationship grew stronger and he noticed my interest in the subject—indeed, my appetite for it—he grew bolder and more varied in his tales. Every day he came up with another story that effectively synopsized a new state of affairs, a lay of the land that I knew nothing about due to my experience—basically, null and void—in this area. With the onrush, the exploding diversity, of his accounts, I noticed that he, too, was getting a lot of pleasure out of the telling. The sort of pleasure you'd get if you'd never had sex at all.

As for Ramadan's poetry: because of the weightiness it posed relative to the audience at No. 36, and due also to the general lack of appropriate publishing opportunities for classical monorhyme odes—for the pretenders of modernism were on patrol, as he always would say with a heartfelt expulsion of breath—he was persuaded that the channel presenting itself for propagating his poetry was the school. And that outlet offered him an audience that Egypt's most famous poets weren't lucky enough to have. During the morning lineup, when all the students stood waiting in the yard, he delighted the ears of teachers and pupils alike with those poems that were eminently acceptable to the censorship board. He did not let a single social or national political or even global occasion pass without embracing it poetically. He wrote on feast days and seasons and the Palestine issue and the tragedy of the Iraqi people our brethren, and Di's fatal accident and the assassination of Laurent Kabila and the birth of Dolly the ewe. Sometimes in these poems he availed himself of symbols or went so far as to offer a trenchant critique of general conditions, and in addition he lampooned certain personalities, in particular, the Superintendent, his wife, and Abu Gamal.

In class, after really closing the door, he disseminated his libertine poems to the students.

But it wasn't enough to circulate his poetry through recitation. The Prof always annexed to his declamations a finely tuned exegesis, clarifying the circumstances of each poem's emergence into the world, expounding on literary techniques and content. Thus, for this poem, *the poet found his inspiration in the loud agonies of his fellow citizens and in their multitudinous suffering, and so it came to him lofty and loud in tone as befits the tumult of the voice of the broad masses; it is a relentlessly savage response to the nonsense of the poets of modernism who for imperialist aims persist in separating poetry from the sources that inspire it hidden as they are within the gentle folded wings of the masses.* And the next poem *gushes from the depths of the poet's blood where lies his own particular and most personal experience and so it emerges with a whisper, warm, like the rustling of the trees that adorn the banked surfaces of our mighty river.*

Although in most circumstances Ustadh Ramadan finds it beneath him to participate in mass public poetry readings or to make appearances in the gatherings of literary lions, we should note that he was a shining star in the sole poetry performance in which he did take part. That's because during it occurred an incident that constituted the most important event of his life bar none, and he confronted this event with a strength drawn solely from his respect for History, to the point that he *felt in his body the flash of History's cameras as they recorded his every gesture.* That's why he tried his utmost to be precise and sharp and decisive, when he sounded forth from the depths of the recital hall: "*Stop!* This ode is not your ode! Pilferer! Pi-i-lfe-e-r-er!!"

At the podium stood a poet from the hinterland, declaiming a heroic battleground poem. When he heard Prof Ramadan's shriek, he paused in complete disarray. He began to sweat visibly and he made to leave the podium. This gave the Professor the opening he needed to take command of the situation, and moreover to resume his history lesson. "Stay right where you are!" he shouted again, and in his stentorian voice he picked up the recitation where the poet had left off, declaiming the very ode. The hall broke into a tumult of sharp applause to which the Professor bowed several times. In a voice choked up by the occasion, he uttered words of emotive power that deserved truly to be recorded in the protocols of history as a guide and light for coming generations . . . and he said nothing at all about the poem's rightful place among his own collected works.

5

People are delighted—in the normal course of events—when they hear the news that a pious man has been caught red-handed in some wrongful act, whether a sin divinely prohibited, a scandalous act undermining the gravity and might of his religiosity, or an error that strips from him the cloak of infallibility to expose him as an ordinary person who doesn't carry the halo of sainthood after all. Perhaps they react this way because his commitment to virtue has been wounding their consciences; perhaps it's a question of seeking psychological equilibrium. It's a relief to be able to rely on the sins of a man who appears close to God in coming to terms with their own sins, which they suspect are quite appalling, and they can think optimistically about committing other wrongs that are no less atrocious. Or maybe it's because people generally find it hard to put up with individuals who lay it on thick when it comes to virtue and commitment— their own as well as what they advise others to acquire.

When Abu Gamal revealed Shaykh Hasan's secret to the residents of No. 36, every one of them immediately acquired the glazed aura of someone who has worked really hard to obtain something and suddenly finds it right in front of him. Postponing their battles, they freed themselves completely to swap versions of the ins and outs of this secret narrative. What's more, they built up every aspect, each according to his whims and the powers of his imagination, for it seems this was the appropriate and satisfying response to his counsels which had been unending.

Shaykh Hasan is from Sohag. It was there that he did the heinous deed. He slept with his mother-in-law. Afterward the remorse nearly killed him. He contemplated suicide down to the details, but he discovered that he wasn't strong enough to face death, and so he decided to turn for help to the people of knowledge and learning. He took up his bundle and turned his face to Cairo. Specifically, his goal was the Azhar, noble seat of Islamic learning, and a fatwa that would put his conscience at rest. He sought a crutch in his defective piety, a definitive jurisprudential opinion to end his mortal confusion. Waiting for the legal greybeard to whom he would present his woeful case, he met Abu Gamal, who was there on a similar mission.

Or two missions. The first was wicked, and he really should be ashamed. He was in search of a misstep Gamal might possibly have made, in order to break his lousy pride and rub his nose in the muddy pit of immorality. Gamal, after all, was living with his wife Hanan even though he had sworn aloud a third time (thus, irrevocably) that he was divorcing her. The second mission was an errand of goodness and charity: to obtain a fatwa legalizing his anticipated grandson, who had now completed his eighth month in Nahid's belly, for Salah had married her after . . . after what? Let it be "after the pen fell into the inkwell" so as not to anger the censors. In her fourth month of expecting the now-anticipated grandson, Nahid was wed to Salah with all due ceremony.

In front of the *faqih*'s door, like invalids exchanging complaints about their ailments as they await the doctor, each con-

fided his problem to the other but with a minor alteration to protect themselves against embarrassment. Abu Gamal thus laid his
children's problems at the door of the household directly across
the street, and it was his good fortune that one of the building
owner's sons was also a Gamal. "He's an old man, poor geezer, so
I said to myself (Abu Gamal told Hasan), I'll do this and gain
some credit in heaven. I'll come see if I can find him an answer to
this calamity he's got in his boys. . . . One jumped on top of a
good girl from a good family before he married her, the other
one's sleeping with his wife while God frowns on him."

Hasan, for his part, made up a friend and transferred the burden to his shoulders. "Came begging me for this favor after that
awful thing he done, can you believe the cheek?"

Even with the unmistakable ring of sincerity and concern,
each man suspected the other was lying. On leaving the graybeard's cubbyhole they confirmed it. Abu Gamal came out
prancing, rejoicing aloud that he'd hit upon a loophole in the
eyes of God with which he could buy the obeisance of his unco-
operative son, and an unambiguous fatwa that his awaited grandson was clear and away legitimate in God's eyes. In Shaykh
Hasan's case, on the other hand, it was his tears and the bewilder-
ment attending his search for a place of shelter in Cairo now that
a return to Sohag was clearly impossible that gave him away.
Since the only soul he knew in this city was Abu Gamal, he asked
whether his new friend knew *any place he could hide himself until
Our Lord smoothed things out.* To tempt Abu Gamal into helping
him, Hasan launched into his tale again. He told the whole thing
a second time, but with perfect honesty this time, no alterations
implicating friends. Abu Gamal was so much affected by the
story that he burst into sobs and threw himself and all he pos-
sessed into succoring this man (for it's generally true that people

are enthusiastic about helping those who are weaker than they are, probably so that they can establish firmly, to their own satisfaction, that they are indeed strong). Abu Gamal made him a promise in the manner of loyal men. "That secret of yours—it'll stay deep in the well, fella! Even if this business of finding you a spot means I have to dissolve a contract, change rooms around . . . my man, I'll put you in two rooms and a sitting room facing north, and don't worry about a thing in the world. From this day on consider yourself just like my children. . . . What's the world come to now—just keep in mind, now, your Lord is the Patient One when it comes to making a mistake, and He's the Veiler of All Deeds, too."

Hasan entered No. 36 in Abu Gamal's grip and under his protection. He moved into the apartment that the Prof has his eyes on now. From day one he and Gamal loathed each other mutually and equally for reasons that were obscure, and he gave free rein to his beard so that he could become Shaykh Hasan. "Allah" and "the Prophet" were always on his tongue now, and he was careful to keep to himself and to avoid any impurities from the house to the mosque, and from the mosque to his work. No pals, no wasting time in coffeehouses, and he left no opportunity to seize upon a good deed left unexploited, especially if it was an opportunity that imposed no burden. In his opinion, a good deed offers a kind of bank account susceptible to eternal growth. For lo, the good deed is like ten of its kind.[1] And Allah gives great increase for whomsoever He wishes.[2] And, according

1. Qur'an 6.160: "Whoever brings a good deed will receive tenfold its like."

2. Qur'an 2.261. This diction also occurs elsewhere in the Qur'an; but punishment can also be "increased" (e.g., Qur'an 11.20, 25.69).

to him, a good deed equals its weight in gold—even one good deed, for every good deed is a generous step toward the blessings of Paradise, bringing him closer to heaven while at the same time putting distance between him and the inferno of his accursed secret, in this world and the hereafter.

And as the Shaykh's wealth expanded, his fear of poverty underwent rampant inflation. The study of poverty now engrossed him.

Abu Gamal kept abreast of Shaykh Hasan's every step with great admiration, and likely a measure of envy and distress, too, for the Shaykh seemed to embody the ideal son for whom Abu Gamal had fervently hoped—"instead of Gamal over there, who befriends anyone and everyone and throws his money around for no good reason."

First, Shaykh Hasan got work at the Helwan Silk Factory as a result of a nice, artery-clogging supper Abu Gamal stuffed into the Director of Employee Affairs. But in short order and for two reasons he left the factory. One reason was hereafterish and the other was quite worldly. In the first case, the Shaykh's shift got in the way of the Five Daily Prayers. In the second case, the work itself didn't mesh with his ambitions for independence and secretiveness. Everyone, that is, always knew exactly what he was doing. So he turned his sights on commerce. He exploited to the full the possibilities inherent in a certain religious occasion, the Mulid Nabawi—commemoration of the Prophet's Birthday.

Hasan erected a small tent at the entrance to the building and stuffed it full of Mulid sweets, purchased on credit with only a good word to the wholesaler from Abu Gamal as a pledge against payment. As he gave his honorable word to the wholesaler, Abu Gamal also overlooked the expense and trouble he had gone to in providing the artery-clogging supper, which clearly had all been for nothing. Abu Gamal, that is, maintained his manly gallantry at its normally buoyant level.

From the start of his venture Shaykh Hasan upheld the motto of secrecy: "Be Confident, Your Needs Will Be Met Under Cover." And in reality this slogan did not betray him: indeed, it was among the prime factors contributing to his success. After all, if you truly believe that secretiveness is the leading dynamic behind getting your interests in place, then any breach thereto means failure. And this is what Shaykh Hasan avoided absolutely. Therefore, his business succeeded and expanded, the tent turned into a shop with solid walls, and the seasonal Mulid sweets were replaced by foodstuffs in all their variety.

The Shaykh spun a winning number, and his luck played havoc with the relationship cemented by the secret at the door of the graybeard *faqih* in the Noble Azhar. The increase in his monetary fortunes gave Shaykh Hasan a heady feeling of power. He knew for certain now that he had freed himself from the secret that had so disfigured his existence; or let's just say he forgot all about it. Now he shrugged off the stranger's wary remoteness with which he'd led his life, beginning to move about our building and the vicinity as if he were a normal person with the right to voice opinions on whatever went on around him.

Those who are closest have first dibs on our charity, as the religion instructs us. Therefore, one night at the mosque, immediately after the evening prayer, Shaykh Hasan proclaimed that "whosoever witnesses an act prohibited by the faith will change it by his own hand. And 'prohibited,' my brethren, describes exactly what Brother Gamal is doing, for he cohabits with his wife against God's Law."

Naturally, this announcement was considered a slip of the tongue and no one paid it any mind. Nasser's Newtown was more like a village than it was a seamless part of the capital city; and in the end, its longtime residents (Abu Gamal, for instance) were family; moreover, they were workmates in the factories of Helwan; and every household knew exactly how far the secrets of every other household went and kept them carefully under wraps. No one had the slightest tolerance for a stranger entering their midst to create scandal in this way.

Of course, the loud silence that greeted his rhetoric more than sufficed to convince Hasan to forget his carefully laid strategy for raiding the bango sessions in Gamal's apartment. Abu Gamal, however, did not forget. He neither forgot Hasan's proclamation nor considered it a slip of the tongue. And to express just how much it meant to him he began to poke at that old secret, to rejuvenate it in his memory, like a rusty weapon that you clean so that you can avail yourself of it at any moment. The stranger whom he had taken in with open arms because he'd been so frail and needy had grown strong. He didn't need to be propped up any more. Therefore one was duty-bound, in present circumstances, to seek out the appropriate means of causing him harm (for, according to Abu Gamal, people are of two sorts: either weak, and to be succored with all in one's possession, or strong, to be enfeebled in any way one can manage). Affectionate sympathy became doubt that quickly crystallized into patent hatred, sparked especially when his recollection of the secret in all its particulars led him to observe that Shaykh Hasan had imposed the law of silence on him even though he—Abu Gamal—*had zealously undertaken to succor him in a moment of crying need.*

So Abu Gamal followed precedent and resorted first to the

mosque ("may we escape all affliction, it's the Lord's house, belongs to everyone"). After evening prayer he broadcast Hasan's secret, without prejudice, in equal measure to all believers. He returned home bent on throwing the bastard out despite entreaties from all, including even Gamal himself.

"He's an immoral cheat and I'm afraid for my boys' women."

And because, when all was said and done, the Shaykh was a stranger and an outsider, what Abu Gamal said was not taken as a mere slip of the tongue. The people of Manshiyat Nasir refused to host the Shaykh even until the next morning. He left the house and the neighborhood, never to return.

In the apartment under the stairs, beneath Hasan's apartment (newly occupied by the Prof), lived the Doctoress. She was a nurse who had deserted her profession upon discovering that serving in family households was more fruitful and more restful, especially since she chose the homes of actresses. She began with the pioneers of Arabic theater, moved on to more recent generations, and settled ultimately in the domicile of Yusra, contemporary star of stage and screen. In her leisure hours—of which she had many, thanks to the out-of-town travel schedules characteristic of actresses—the Doctoress augmented her income by obliging those who wanted to sleep with her in exchange for her own officially set, noninflationary rate, which she tried seriously to keep within reasonable bounds for local consumption, following state practice to protect citizens against price gouging, each according to his ability to pay. Village rates for the yokels, city rates for townies. As for non-Egyptian Arab guests, here she earned in dollars on a sliding scale calibrated to the customer's conditions and age. In both cases, domestic and foreign, her trade was profitable. It's true that she wasn't pretty enough to really *seduce* customers, but she was well aware of her body's aptitudes. She knew she had a body that gave off an unusual aura of mystery, inducing an immediate reaction in any man who caught a glimpse of her.

The Doctoress was a native of Qena, daughter of an ex-worker whose fame still reverberated since his name had been given to one of those enormous industrial machines as an expression of condolence after the goliath had ground him into hamburger. The soul of the martyred worker moved on to its heavenly glories and the Doctoress moved on to live with her sister, who had to kick her out after catching her husband flat on his stomach in front of the bathroom door trying to get a look at her body's secret as she bathed. So the *Doktoora* relocated, naming a fairly impressive number of houses in the Manshiya among her residential addresses. In the end, she stood in the street before Abu Gamal, who promptly gave her the stairwell apartment. For she fulfilled the two historic conditions in the absence of which Abu Gamal does not agree to house a stranger. The applicant must be his compatriot from the Said, Egypt's south—a real *Abu baladiyyat*—and must in addition suffer from some affliction or disability, which category could include a woeful mistake that person might have happened to make. The affliction had to appeal to Abu Gamal's sensibility and his sympathies for it served as his guarantee of the new resident's fealty and—with the first wrong move—as a weapon effectively brandished. Shaykh Hasan he chucked out by means of the secret; in Prof Ramadan's case, he was keeping tabs on the rumor that the Prof had raped one of his female students. In my case he had diddled with the rental contract for my apartment in a way that made it very easy to throw me out. With Adil, "being a Koftes" was enough to satisfy Abu Gamal.

When Abu Gamal had made sure the Doctoress was comfortable in her surroundings, he zeroed in on the subject of the customers. "The building's secure. No need for the hassle and expense of a short-term rent outside of here, and I'll go easy. See, we split it." To tempt her he sketched out a plan ensuring a twofold benefit: preserving his establishment's reputation, and enabling her revenge on the sister who had chased her out.

They began operations at once. The Doctoress acquired her sister's husband as an ordinary customer. No sooner did her labor commence in the stairwell apartment than who should make an appearance but Abu Gamal, with the sister in hand. Divorce was followed by blessed marriage, God willing . . . and the Doctoress's union to her sister's newly ex-husband was feted in the stairwell apartment and things were moving along just about perfectly toward consummation of the scheme's projected success. The husband was quick to adopt a practical attitude. In fact, he found the whole idea to his liking, being satisfied to have one day in return for a decent sum amounting to precisely a third of the takings. The customers divided up the rest of the week. Abu Gamal organized and supervised and kept watch over the proceedings. Then all of a sudden Gamal popped up in the midst of their maneuvers and spoiled everything. The Doctoress took his fancy. He began laying the foundations for an assignation, following his usual and well-known blueprint.

It was certainly within the Doctoress's capabilities to handle Gamal as a normal customer, thereby preserving the whole scheme (especially since Gamal was prepared to pay on the spot). But here was this sudden and elusive feeling that this was the man she'd been looking for all her life. She also sensed that the stories Gamal told were rebuking her, somehow. They made her feel low . . . forced her to remember that she was available . . . that she was a whore . . . and she screamed. "What's happened, you stinking pimp! You've been treating me just like the sleazy broads you're always sweet-talking. Well I'm the *Doktoora,* and don't you forget it!"

Even though the incident caused Abu Gamal to wish permanent blindness on his son, at the same time he felt his manhood sorely tested and somehow insulted by her rebuff of his son. He made the sacrifice of ditching the whole scheme and initiated proceedings to throw out the Doctoress. He called together all his sons, including Gamal, who naturally expressed heroic zeal for this venture, and together they made for the stairwell.

It was a raging battle indeed. The Doctoress exhibited rare courage and would have come out victorious had it not been that Gamal noticed, while exchanging kicks, that her breasts were unsupported by a bra. He found it a perfect opportunity to kill two birds with one stone. The family would come out on top, and he would strike a blow in defense of his own dethroned masculinity. He fastened on hard to her breasts and did not let go until she announced her surrender and agreed to leave the house.

the newborn was a male coming into a family moving slowly from Bedouin to peasant life.

I was in that vanguard of Bedouin offspring who weren't ashamed of tending the remnants of their land—our vast lands, granted to our ancestors by the Ottoman Viceroy Muhammad Ali Pasha early in the nineteenth century. This was one of the preferential treatments doled out to Egypt's nomads, but it was like donating a slaughtered beast to a gaggle of hungry men in a desert without teaching them the skill of skinning it. The recipients were as bound to let the tracts fragment through inheritance as they were likely to hand it out to chance passersby. They left their deserts to enter this unfamiliar terrain in a state of disarray, lost beneath the weight of their tents. They poured in as if this were the aftermath of a successful raid, as if they'd forced the government into a truce with a ransom they had no idea was valuable. They settled down exactly as Muhammad Ali intended them to, but they remained loyal to the principle that planting and tending the land they'd been granted was beneath their dignity, and they were delighted to barter it away for the most worthless trifle. Nor did they cease their nomadic life. They simply narrowed the confines of their seasonal migrations, staying within the boundaries of their new entitlement.

Naturally, the remnants of land that my generation inherited were confined indeed, and their borders did press too tightly upon us. And so, unhappily, we were forced to plant the remaining land. We didn't do so as the peasants we were supposed to be but rather as part-time farmers who took enormous care to preserve those aspects of nomadic identity in which the pure Bedouin invests such fierce pride. A fellow owning one paltry acre that would barely keep him if he planted the whole expanse

6

On the 16th of August 1998, I entered No. 36, Street 14, Manshiyat Nasir, Helwan, for the first time. It was a hot day, normal for August, its heat reminding me now and then that I'd come into the world on a similar day about thirty years before: to be exact, on the 16th of August 1968.

In celebration of that occasion—and I'm still trying to figure out where I stand on it—I picture my mother's face, which must have been layered in sweat as I slipped out of her on such a flaming hot day.

Always, whenever I recall this day, my imagination pauses at the beads of sweat pouring down my mother's face. Perhaps it's a longing to bestow some measure of suffering or gravity or wonder on the event of my birth, even though it's a perfectly ordinary thing, drops of sweat—big ones, even—across the face of a woman in childbirth. It's to be expected. True, I'm my mother's tenth and final child, which without a doubt made the task easier. Since my way had been prepared—once my nine siblings, who were of varying sizes, had widened the lane properly—I must have made the trip easily, without any hitches, maybe even yawning all the way. But surely it wasn't a moment devoid of aches and pains. We were in the hottest month of the year, and would split it in half and then sell one of the halves in order to buy a stallion whose pedigree he could boast of and a rifle to keep folks in awe. The other half he wouldn't be ashamed of farming.

Maybe this was why I was so good at concluding truces with everyone in sight. Thus, when I'm among our historic and mortal enemies, the settled farmer population, I exude the image of a poor wretch just going about my own business meekly. Among my own people, though, I'm a Bedouin whose eyes give off sparks. With my ability to move from one to the other, when I came to Cairo I didn't encounter any problems of the sort that earlier fellows coming from the villages and tiny settlements faced. I took up residence on the city's fringe, while at its heart I racked up some splendid-looking successes.

When I was a construction worker, I acquired more than a little renown in the scruffy little cafes where day-labor contractors collected. I was one of those heavy-duty toughs you could depend on when a job meant shifting sacks of sand, cement, and gravel, or meters of tiling, to the highest floors—on the shoulders of the guys you hired, so that you could dispense with modern means of heavy lifting. Even while my soul was at death's door beneath the weight of those sacks, I didn't lack for the occasion to feel awed by the unending pride I took in my sterling Bedouin tribe, which had left the government no choice but to make peace with it.

❧ I helped to raise an incredible number of buildings throughout various districts of Cairo. This gave me a strong sense of self-accomplishment whenever I happened to pass by one of these buildings, and soon the time came for me to think about rising in my profession. I looked forward to a future in which I would be one of the building contractors. And since a contractor has to have an established address, one that his customers come to know, I had to say good-bye to the rented rooms in which construction workers lived. There was no permanence to these lodgings because they were always attached in some fashion to unfinished buildings whose owners were trying to get them finished. And finishing them meant that the workers had to search for another windowless basement hole attached to a building that wasn't yet finished . . .

I spent a day laboring hard with the apartment broker. Our day drew to a close in front of a suitable third-floor apartment with a north-facing balcony. I was on the point of taking it, but in the midst of negotiations with the owner I became aware that the overall appearance of the building wasn't very reassuring. A heavy odor hung over it, and the stairs had never breathed in the smell of paint. So I held back.

Not for my own sake. Anyone who has spent a decade living in rented rooms in unfinished buildings is certainly not going to howl about niceties like the lack of paint or whitewash on the staircase to an apartment that he is going to inhabit—*a whole apartment!* No, it was for the sake of the sons of the tribe. I had been so fixated on improving my life, once I was in the city, having left the Bedouin settlements truly behind, that I had lied about a few things, especially my material circumstances. So it would have been inconceivable for them to imagine I would live in such a rundown place. This truly made my situation a sensitive one, which I described to the broker in great detail and emotionally, I guess, since my agitation produced an effect. Here he was patting me on the shoulder and urging, "Don't worry. No problem. No problem at all," while I was having trouble keeping the tears back. To stay ahead of me, before I could burst into sobs he took me along Street 14 and stopped me as we faced No. 36. "It's a bit high," he said. "It'll cost you. But it would do you proud."

Proud indeed. It was a distinguished building, five stories high. The distinctive overhang of the balcony, jutting out further than any other edifice on this street, gave it a commanding presence that tipped you off to its inhabitants' uniquely striking characters. The facade was green and marked out by ornamental squares of a more intense green. The strategic zone had been sprinkled down, and against the wall was tipped a chair befitting a fairly commanding backside. From above the door stared the head of a wild animal, its mouth open in a savage grin, its teeth so sharp you couldn't but feel that the blood still ran steaming through its veins.

"Juicy green prospects tonight, God willing," said the broker, and entered. I didn't hold back hesitantly as I usually did. I followed him right in, even though the situation demanded some serious thought. It wasn't that the house didn't please me. It did, and my pleasure in it was fueling a growth in the total sum required for one apartment, before my very eyes. That's why.

The broker stopped in front of an apartment on the third floor. His tone of voice was one that the term "polite" wouldn't begin to convey. I added this observation immediately to the balconies' prominent aspect over the street, on my register of the owner-occupiers' public weight.

"Hagg Abu Gamal."

His call was ignored, which gave me a chance to study the staircase. It was a broad sweep of stairs with a pleasing appearance

marred only by the overly long run of stairs before the first landing. Someone had wanted the two ground-floor doors to be visible from the front entrance, and so a single, long flight of stairs
led to the next floor rather than a more architecturally sensible
two flights with a landing between, one of which would have
necessarily saddled the two ground-floor apartment doors with
bulky ceiling supports.

"Hagg Abu Gamal?"

"Come on in, Abu Ahmad! Welcome, welcome—make
yourself at home."

"Customer with me."

To hear myself called "customer" suddenly made me uncomfortable. A man between fifty and sixty years old emerged.
His vast paunch didn't hide the reality of his brawn. Clearly, he
was an exercise buff of some sort.

"What's the matter, Abu Ahmad? Cat got your tongue?" He
favored me with a smile that I accepted with a more or less con-
trite nod.

"Welcome, now . . . you from the south, or the Delta?"

I remembered facing questions like this once when the loss
of my identity card led to my admittance as a guest of the residents of Pyramids Police District prison, the only difference
being that those questions had been accompanied then by hard
slaps to the back of my neck that were impressive enough that I
was reluctant to answer. I don't know why I expected Abu
Gamal to do the same thing. From the way he phrased the question, I knew he belonged to our brothers the Saidis, those south-
erners who are constitutionally suspicious when it comes to sons
of the north, perhaps in fear of them. So I said with a swagger,
"No problem—from the South, for sure."

"You're coming to live here with us, then. Welcome, welcome!" He gave me a vigorous handshake that would do a sports hero proud, obliging me to feel the value of living in his home. He pulled me inside and I found myself surrounded by the building's most reverend, august presences . . .

- Gamal "Good Looks" Abd al-Halim
- Sayf "the Sword" Abd al-Halim
- Salah "Piety and Probity" Abd al-Halim
- and Amer "Thriving" Abd al-Halim

. . . since just then they were all gathered in the apartment of their father, the Hagg Abd al-Halim. I learned later that this rare meeting had been called for the purpose of terrorizing Shaykh Hasan. For the day I entered that house was precisely the day he left it.

❧ From the beginning of my residence at No. 36, I wasn't troubled by Sayf's incessant borrowing. He demanded only trivial sums, and I considered this a reasonable fee to pay for access to whatever family secrets I could easily access. For there was a sense in which I remained a stranger, and an outsider always suffers from a dearth of information, which means he continues to be an outsider, which turns his life into one long and ever-renewed fear of the others. The farther you are from the secrets of those others, the more mysterious and unclear is their power, and the stronger grows your fear of their capacities for evil.

My relationship with Sayf was one of mutuality. It was based on a goal that was clear, real, and perpetual—swapping my personal interest for his. He suffered from insolvency and I craved more secrets. He was bent on keeping the relationship going and he knew the importance of what he was offering. He revealed family secrets only to the measure of the precise sum he was seeking. And I was determined not to overdo my generosity so that he would be driven to go further, extending the relationship and endlessly remaking it.

The first secret Sayf considered appropriate to pass to me—in exchange for five pounds—was that Um Gamal, his mother, had opposed my moving in because I was unmarried, and "the house is full of women in heat." This was a valuable secret—obviously—and it led me to anticipate a brilliant future in this house.

Among the building's residents, Um Gamal was the only one I'd failed utterly to form clear and decisive feelings about. At this stage I hadn't yet managed to see her in person. But her voice was a pretty good way to start making her acquaintance—an aural acquaintance closely correlated with the dirty words she flung at her daughters-in-law, which began her morning and left their distinct impression on my ears. Um Gamal's language on these occasions was sexually explicit and selected carefully for maximum impact, and as she spoke she acted out her words with gestures so faithful and so fluent as to strip her utterances of the crudeness such swearwords normally carry, removing all suggestion of shamefulness and obliging you to accept them as dialogue from an ordinary scene which Um Gamal had a perfect right to perform on her chosen stage—the street—and in front of a not inconsiderable number of spectators. Furthermore, she embellished her delivery with fragments drawn from her family's history—a history insistently denied to have any flaw, any blemish, any stain that might curtail its venerable origins and its brilliance, with a vehemence that would convince you in and of itself that this was a pretty lowly family. After all, when you bring up something in order to deny it, in some sense you're confirming it.

Um Gamal wakes early, as old folks tend to do (in fact, she was not old in the conventional sense, but I prefer to keep her old). And once she is up, it's impossible to get any more sleep. In celebration of a new day's dawning, she chatters with children, cats and garbage, and has words with the guy who sells rotting *ful* and tomatoes, regardless of whether the price is a little steep today or whether she can get them cut-rate. Her yakking leaves no room for doubt that it's meant to annoy you. That's not her overt intention, of course. It's just that she is suspicious of anyone who isn't a morning person. Or perhaps she is exercising her right to summon others to share her joy at the new day.

At that stage, the image I had of her form resembled the megaphone which people used to place on the highest roof in our tiny settlement as they made preparations to commemorate someone's death—or the specific megaphone through which Shaykh Husni scandalized the entire neighborhood of Imbaba in the film *Kit Kat*. The base of this megaphone was very narrow while the front section was incredibly wide. But it was the garbage bag that put an end to my auditory image of Um Gamal and gave me a prime opportunity to see her face-to-face.

I was carrying the garbage bag down the stairs when I caught sight of her in the stairwell—just a glimpse, but it revealed how very closely imagination can match the real thing. There was something about Um Gamal that made me think of that nurse Raskolnikov killed in *Crime and Punishment*. A behind that was really miniature, one surely faced with a dilemma beneath the weight of Abu Gamal, and a chest of proportions the generosity of which you can fully appreciate and properly laud only after you have heard the magnificent voice it produces. In the course of my bewildered and desperate attempt to find safe passage past her, I made it down to the second floor, my eyes fixed on the ground as if I were looking for something. Why, I don't know, but even to come face-to-face with her seized me with something like embarrassment or fear. I supposed she was heading upward toward me, so I stopped and began to reverse direction toward my apartment. She surprised me by smacking herself across her chest so forcefully that it caused me pain: "SHAMEFUL, MY BOY, COMING DOWN YOURSELF TO THROW OUT THE GARBAGE!" In a voice defined by its quaver, she ordered me to consider her my mother and not take out the garbage myself. Period. I was to leave it by the door to my apartment, "and any one of those damned bitch bombshells can take it outside." And so the very next day I started thinking of her as my mother and I left the garbage bag by my door, and when I met her face-to-face on the flight of stairs coming down to the second floor, I flashed her a smile suitable for mothers. The moment I'd successfully squeezed past her, though, her voice punctured my eardrum. "BROTHER YOU'VE MADE THE WHOLE HOUSE STINK! LEAVING YOUR GARBAGE OUT IN FRONT OF YOUR DOOR LIKE THAT— YOU THINK WE'RE YOUR SERVANTS OR SOMETHING? ALLAH! THAT SAYING IS SO TRUE, 'SHY TO ACT, DIES FOR A FACT.'"

All night long Um Gamal pleads with God, faithfully and earnestly, to arrange things so that she will wake up as a man. And then she wakes up very early to find that she is as she ever was, Um Gamal, daughter of the first wife of a man who married seven women in order to prove to his first wife that she was the cause of his begetting daughter after daughter. Truly, God granted him success in his endeavors, for the youngest wife gave birth to five hefty men, and she—the first—died saying with confidence befitting the wise, "Everyone who was ever wronged has enjoyed our Lord's revenge on the wrongdoer—except for me. From the day that man left me, he never came back even to see the girl."

Um Gamal wasn't the only daughter of this wife whose revenge God put off until later. All the while she was looking hard for a baby boy there slipped out of her, after Umm Gamal, two daughters all in one blow, who departed this life swiftly, not because their births were difficult but because after the placenta was removed and buried in the ground, their mother left the door to their navels ajar. The thread with which the midwife had tied their cords broke, and they died at once.

The ease of this method for getting rid of two daughters gave Naqawa strong regrets. Not because she had gotten rid of her daughters at the moment of their birth, but rather because she had not gotten rid of Um Gamal by the same method. She would announce her regret to Um Gamal, honestly and sincerely, like a courageous general embracing his one remaining soldier after losing the battle.

"Aaah, *ya binti,* if only your navel had split open as your sisters' did, your father wouldn't a' left us and folks wouldn't have messed around with us, no respect, no money, nothin' left, people insulting us as much as they liked."

"*Ya mama,* you had two more after me—so if he was gonna marry, he'd marry no matter what."

"So what, I had girls—once they were dead its like I didn't even have a baby, period, so he would've stayed on with me till our Lord release all."

Old Naqawa's regret was like the remorse of another Naqawa. But *this* "Purity" was a select part of my family's heritage. She was the first of my great-grandfather Saqr's wives, and she gave birth to a boy. That was my grandfather Isa. No more children arrived. One day my great grandfather returned from his migration to the pastureland, taking his time . . . and with a young girl behind him.

"Who's this, Saqr?"

"This one? She'll help you around the house and fill the place with babies' cries."

"Where'd you find her?"

"Girl belongs to some scum I found at the well."

I didn't know who they were, those weaklings whose daughter my great-grandfather took as if he were making off with one of their sheep, but what is common knowledge is that this young thing didn't stop having boys. My great-grandmother snatched every one of those boys as soon as he slid out to deliver him safely to his prescribed fate, plunging into his soft cranium a needle she'd kept beneath her own head ever since my great-grandfather had returned home with his new wife. Though it was a needle meant for mending tents, it had the honor of roving the depths of five heads brought forth by my great grandmother's co-wife. The sixth was saved for a simple reason, which was that my great-grandmother was otherwise occupied and elsewhere. At the time of his birth, she and my great-grandfather were performing their religious duty as pilgrims to Mecca. Since that was way back when people went on the Hajj by camel, they were away for so many months that the baby's skull had time to harden. So his head withstood the needle and he grew up with his elder half-brother.

And much later, when the sons of the tribe of al-Basil struck my grandfather Isa and broke open his skull, the sixth one—his brother—attacked them. Being extremely handy with his stick, he bashed in their heads, every one, in front of my great-grandmother's eyes. Unable to contain herself, she shrieked, "Your hand be blessed . . . the day of the needle is undone!" She turned immediately to my great-grandfather and, out there in front of everyone, she confessed to those crimes committed by the needle. He killed her. He killed her then and there.

7

As in the histories of ancient empires—especially those of the East—the sons of remote hamlets like ours went through three stages sexually. First, the stage of the young empire's founding, vigorous and strong; usually this stage would be full of mistakes and excesses that went along with establishing an empire out of nothing. Second, the golden age, in which the empire reaches the height of its glory and its furthest reach. And finally, decline and eclipse at the hands of the last of the family's offspring—child of the dynasty that had built the empire in the first place—who is characteristically incapable and weak-willed.

For me, the first stage was one of clumsy attempts at finding a way to put out the flames that unexpectedly began to rip through my body. I began with the traditional version of the secret act, seeking aid from—or, better, exploiting—the fertility of our land when it came to appropriate vegetation—sesame, *mulukhia* leaves, purslane, the like. But this wore me out. Trying to give form to my imaginings, of course, was like carving rock with a feather, since the details of female anatomy were a mystery to me, so much so that I would imagine—at that moment of ultimate passion—women's bodies with powerful claws emerging from them that I was constantly having to avoid (to this day I can't explain why I was pursued by the issue of claws).

Then I was guided somehow to our donkey. This event had the effect of lifting a heavy burden from my imagination, and thus did the true beginnings of my history come to pass . . . a rip-roaring kickoff that all but felled me with a deadly blow, because she was young, our donkey, and lacked experience, and in any case she wasn't of that breed of donkey characterized by serene equanimity. This became abundantly clear as soon as I tied her up. Or, more accurately, shackled and hobbled her in a hole that I used up an entire day digging. She liberated herself at a moment when I wasn't looking—or rather, was completely absorbed elsewhere—by freeing her left rear leg, the hoof as hard as rock and stronger. Just as I freed myself of my drawers she surprised me with a kick that hit home. I collapsed spectacularly in the way of a guy who knows death is looking him in the face. I moaned and moaned, begging God's forgiveness, *real* forgiveness, sincerely, and I recited aloud all the verses from the Qur'an that I had learnt by heart, since it was completely unsuitable to be meeting God in such circumstances.

It seems that my voice was louder than it should have been for prayer. Here was our neighbor Abd al-Tawwab, who had obviously heard me. Our donkey was crashing into the walls of the crater I had made, like an assaulted girl putting up resistance, and my drawers were dragging alongside her, and I was trying—as much as I could—to cover myself in my *gallabiyya*.

"What's wrong, son?" asked Abd al-Tawwab.

"Stomachache . . . an *awful* stomachache," I moaned, trying to sound like an invalid in pain.

Abd al-Tawwab gave a good look around. *"La ilah ila Allah!"* he proclaimed, finally. "There is no god but God . . . and God help us."

It was in high school—to be precise, freshman year—that the

Golden Age began. I discovered the scenes to be found on television and, occasionally, at the cinema. This cost me a lot of hard work, the least of which was extending my visits to the home of our tiny settlement's only TV owner, managing to stay through "Tonight's Feature Film"—that TV that developed my imagination, scotched forever the issue of claws, and allowed me to make an acquaintance with every one of the film industry's star actresses. Through the good offices of TV I became an expert craftsman of that wondrous and bewitching fusion: Suhayr Zaki's thigh with Su'ad Husni's waist, combined with the curves of a girl I'd seen passing in the street, together with Shadia's chest (in its younger years). I applied all of it carefully to the form of one of my uncle's daughters, the best among them whose body I could call up in some detail from times when I had lain on my tummy or back so that I could transform my imagination into reality (or family). If one of the elements I had appropriated from the television didn't work for me, I replaced it immediately without any disturbance to the procedure I followed daily, so that if (for example) Suad Husni's middle jammed up the works—and generally it seemed it might, especially when the role she was playing was a depressing one—I replaced it with Naima Akif's waist. The only one I wed permanently to my imagination as she was, whole, was Hind Rustum. Fearful of a scandalous failure, in fact, I used to take a full day of R&R in hopes that I would be up to my task of cornering Hind so completely that she couldn't budge in the restricted spaces of my imagination.

The phase of decline and eclipse (as the empire comes under the rule of the ruling family's weakest child) was in its early stages when I encountered Gamal close up. Really, he was a loyal friend I could rely on in times of hardship. It was the morning after my wedding. We had gotten through a long night (my bride and I), during which we strove to fulfill our sacred duty faithfully; or let's just say that we exhausted ourselves without getting the result anticipated from a pair of young newlyweds. A memorable night from which I emerged with new wisdom, the gist of which was that sex is a secret individual pleasure that fizzles completely if anyone shares it with you. If it is true bliss, it's a joy that only reaches its apex when you're alone and immersed in the secret act, for then you're running the whole show yourself without anyone observing. You're a free man, master of your circumstances. If you are a bit tired, for instance, you can simply postpone the whole operation without any twinges of conscience and without the depressing thought that you might not be able to handle it. Or, if you've been yearning for some legendary and insane activity, no one is going to oppose you. Sex is a pleasure to be seized, a stolen and illicit pleasure, and dual participation, meaning wedlock, misplaces its essence when it makes the whole thing a duty. It becomes a nightly battle from which you have to come out victorious, a contest in which your adversary is always stronger . . . through circumcision and through shame, old practices and honor. It all goes to show that we really are pretty pitiful. We always prefer to marry the girl who is honorable, chaste, and sheltered within protective walls, and who has never been through a love story, even though we know *perfectly well* that this girl . . . well, any girl who hasn't flaunted her girlness at the elementary level, fallen in love at the middle-school stage, had sex at the high-school level, and schemed to get an abortion at the university stage must have gone through some major repression of her sex drive.

Gamal came along in the morning to congratulate us on our

felicity in marriage. He took note of my dilemma immediately. To be truthful, it wouldn't have required a particularly keen eye. I was clearly confused and so embarrassed that I asked him at the door, disgust clear in my voice, why the visit? which as far as I was concerned was a surprise. He found himself having to remind me that I had just gotten married. Our relationship—before this visit—hadn't gone beyond run-of-the-mill hellos. But he didn't waste any time on the expected compliments, as he'd come with a specific end in mind. He just said, "Don't worry about it, we've all gone through the same business," and smiled, and before I could get hold of myself and launch into a defense of my manhood, which there was no doubt had been insulted, he added, "Hey, I can spare this, some really good stuff, cost me some trouble to get this opium, Lord! Came my way just yesterday and I was going to have it for the guys coming over tonight but . . . I can see you're a good guy, and a man gets credit above for helping out when it's as bad as this."

And he put a tiny cellophane package down on the table and turned to go. I didn't say a thing, like anyone who's trying to hide something he knows is a disgrace that nothing will explain away. No doubt he'd been spying on us all night long. At the door he lingered. "I know you want me outta here, but just a little advice from your brother. Watch out you don't act like an ass and suck it all in at once—just take off the tiniest sliver, head of a pin—put it under your tongue. You try anything else and I'll know it real fast."

He was an expert. And I had nothing ahead of me but his wrapper. But a need to be my own man made me ignore his counsel, and instead of the head of a pin I inhaled half the chunk. In moments there happened what we'd been searching for all night long, so intensely it shocked even my wife.

8

It's the way words are said that gives them life and defines them as hard or gentle. Words in themselves, without the energy of delivery, are just a string of letters, dead ones that don't mean a thing. Um Gamal's insults, for example, though they were flagrantly sexual, when lobbed into the faces of her sons' wives were delivered with a mildness that attenuated the shameful content, making you hear them more as words of guidance you might well offer to your nearest and dearest without any embarrassment at all.

"*Ghuzza*!" The word was aimed at Amer, and Abu Gamal didn't really mean anything by it. I had heard it time and time again in this house and I always took it as a simple overstatement of things. But this time it was accompanied by a disturbance that suggested something was really wrong and someone had better watch out.

"*Ghuzza*. . . . You'll see the edge of my knife this time! *Ghuzza,* you SON OF A BITCH! I'LL GET YOU THIS TIME!"

Abu Gamal was provoking Amer to go after Hamdi, the bango dealer, who had stopped in front of the house in broad daylight and cursed THE FUCKING FAMILY TREE OF EVERYONE IN THIS GODDAMNED HOUSE, and when Abu Gamal challenged him, he took out his pistol and began shooting. And even though Abu Gamal was spared the bullets, he was struck by something else that he considered more searing than gunfire. In front of the *neighbors*—or the enemies, as he liked to call them—the son of a bitch had said to him, "Hey, pimp, move your backside, go manage your son, will you?"

The evening before, Amer found that he didn't have the money on him for even a pinch of bango. But that didn't keep him from going to Hamdi's den. Instead of money, he prepared something a little different for Hamdi. He got himself an old red mud brick that he stuffed down his back between his belt and his spine so that its bottom third tickled his behind. He hid it all beneath his overcoat. Hamdi handed over the bango as usual. Amer gave it a once-over, stuck his hand into the back pocket of his trousers as if to pull out his wallet, and instead, in one fast and amazing motion, pulled out the brick and whacked Hamdi on the nose hard enough to put him into a coma. Amer took to his heels.

So now here he was considering Abu Gamal's provocation for its practical implications. Hamdi's punishment wouldn't do *him* any good, of course; in fact he might make good use of Hamdi's insult to his father and his shooting at the family home to get his hands on more bango. Not to mention the fact that Amer was perfectly familiar with the principles. As long as he had cracked open the man's nose with the brick—and snitched the bango from under his nose, it was the guy's right to defend his honor. So his thinking went only as far as trying to work out a new method for putting his hands on some bango in coming evenings. Meaning that his thinking didn't go very far at all since it led him only as far as the apartments in this building. . . . Like any man of valor, Amer scorns theft. But sometimes he does resort to it—temporarily and only if circumstances of habit force him into it. And his circumstances weren't so sweet. Prof Ramadan was giving himself over to poetry and so had forgotten his diversion with Zannuba. Gamal, too, was falling into financial straits following a dispute with the counselor, and so that source of occasional fags was no more.

Amer is a very fine-looking guy and is always chic. He's fairly slender—or let's say his build is fragile in some way. But that hasn't kept him from being main man in the youth bango gang, which maintains a good reputation in Manshiyat Nasir and Helwan. Amer's a mechanic (unsuccessful) and a heavy (successful), and not a soul throughout Manshiyat Nasir isn't extremely wary of him. He is distinguished by a type of bravado that you rarely see except perhaps in a wild animal.

Even with his weak build, Amer was always ready to fight the entire street. Yanking off his shirt, he would pound his fists against his unexceptional chest twice, and after that boxing exhibition your only possible reaction was to shrink trembling inside your own skin at the merest glance from him. He maintained a heroic bearing and gallantry you find only in professional criminals, and he was in perpetual quest of a meaning to his masculinity, a meaning obscure even when it came to Amer. The only inkling he had was that it had to do with power, overwhelming force that split people into two categories: valorous men, the victorious; and other-than-men, the defeated.

Aged twenty-two and queued second to last among Abu Gamal's sons, Amer embarked on Life as Gamal's sidekick in the drugs trade. Gamal relied on Amer—so young and energetic—to handle the customer delivery side of the business, plus Amer would always volunteer—for the sake of the business venture—

to test the product *in the customers' presence.* On his rounds, therefore, he toked up in front of the customer until he was shitfaced. It was only logical, then, that the whole scheme gave Amer a second distinction, which was addiction. He had married Zannuba in the traditional way, and their marriage had taken place before he went into the army. But he fled the army to give concrete expression to his love for her.

Because Amer considered thieving from strangers an insult to his manhood he began with his father. The essence of his plan lay in abducting two chickens daily from the poultry farm that Abu Gamal kept on the roof. The price Amer could get for the chickens was the exact equivalent of the cost of a packet of bango. But this didn't last very long since Abu Gamal counted his chickens every day. It didn't take him much sleuthing to discover that the secret of their disappearance lay right in his household. To put a stop to it he made a minor alteration in his sleeping arrangements. He convinced himself that it wouldn't make much of a difference if, instead of slumbering in Um Gamal's embrace, he slept on the rooftop in front of the door to the chicken coop. Amer confronted this modification with one of his own which additionally spared him the tiresome exercise of climbing a whole flight of stairs. Instead of the rooftop he took himself to the apartment of his brother Salah on the fourth floor directly beneath the chicken coop.

Salah's overriding preoccupation was care and recreation of the self. Add to that the fact that joining the Zamalek Sporting Club basketball team allowed him to make all-expenses-paid visits to a selection of the world's states and accustomed him to a style of life he kept to, in part, even after his affliction kept him from pursuing his athletic ambitions. He spent two weeks out of every year on the shores of the Mediterranean in Alexandria, a sacrosanct ritual that eased Amer's path in lifting the contents of his brother's apartment. He began with the videotapes—they were all skin flicks of the worst sort—and next was the video player, which only projected skin anyway; and then, grounding his actions in a consistency (and ease) of purpose, he hauled off the TV. Once he discovered there was no escaping the twinges of his conscience anyway, he felt that he must go ahead and take the cassette recorder, heater, fan, and iron. And then, towering before him, was the fridge: grudgingly, he sought the help of two gang members and they lugged it out the day before Salah's and Nahid's return from their *bon voyage*.

I couldn't help but admire this resounding success, and so fervently did I admire it that my emotions goaded me into searching for a way to rescue my apartment from the same fate. By the rule of logical succession, after all, my place was the next candidate for theft. For one thing, it was directly beneath Salah's apartment. And—in the end—we were family.

First I established the location where Amer was likeliest to launch his assault. If I were in his shoes, I thought, I would pick the bathroom window. It was large, and right next to it climbed a pipe that was perennially broken. That pipe was in constant need of a repairman if the foundations of the house were to remain firm. That is, if I were to return home unexpectedly, he'd have an unassailable pretext for his presence there. The problem with the bedroom window, from Salah's perspective, was that it was narrow, but just to be sure I blocked it, moving the wardrobe in front of it to avoid any naughtiness there.

I always think I could have been a professional thief, a seasoned, smooth thief who stages stunning victories. I'm not talking about those low-down, pathetic burglars who fall back on elementary and undemanding gambits (thuggery plain and simple). Those folks aren't thieves, they're lunatics, and their natural habitat is an asylum, not prison. The thief I had in mind would be a conceptual thinker, a true intellectual, indeed a genius of a thief whose only motive is the pure pleasure of setting in motion and seeing through his shrewd schemes which require efforts far beyond the value of whatever it is he is bent on thieving. His end isn't what he steals but the very act of thievery. If you're him you want to experience that delectable sensation that you're someone. To know you're important enough that people are in hot pursuit. That you've hoodwinked them. You've hypnotized them and gotten hold of what you wanted while continuing to hold onto their inflated regard for you.

I considered fixing steel grates over all the windows and doors, but these are traditional barriers that are effective only in the case of nondomestic thieves. Metal barriers of this sort don't offer resistance to landlord thieves because they always have ample time to dismantle them. That's why I immediately implemented the live electric wiring scheme. Everything proceeded smoothly and simply. I loaded every window with voltage enough to flatten an elephant. Hoping for a trial run, I made sure to inform everyone in the building that these days I wasn't spending much time in my apartment. But my surveillance of the wiring grew long and tedious long before I was able to witness how useful it could be in a real-life situation. True, it was very successful when it came to flattening the rats and frying the insects, and it nearly turned me into a corpse. But what I really wanted was to test its impact on thieves. Real thieves.

9

The Leader—Gamal Abd al-Nasir—paid a surprise visit to one of the factories his Revolution had established in Helwan. He found that an enormous number of its workers were spending all night in the factory. Delighted with their extraordinary self-sacrifice in the cause of labor, he went up to one of them and pumped his hand with obvious enthusiasm. "Good going, keep it up, hero!"

The man tried to plant a kiss on his palm. "God protect you, Pasha. . . . Abdel Halim Abdel Halim here."

"So you're working two shifts, then!"

Trying to respond as he thought the Leader would want, the man said, "God's truth, Pasha, just one shift. Your honor."

"Then why aren't you going home?"

"Where'm I gonna go, Pasha?"—addling the Leader, who had supposed the workers were sleeping in the factory because they were so keen to keep on working, night and day. Surely not because they couldn't find a place to live. For the sake of safe-guarding his Revolution, the Leader waved toward a vacant stretch that happened to be within eyesight.

"Let them live there!" And the workers rushed forward in a perfect likeness of Revolutionary zeal, toward the empty zone. It was a mere matter of days before Manshiyat Gamal Abd al-Nasir—Nasser's Newtown—entered the world.

On its eastern rim the Leader's Newtown is hemmed in by high-tension wires that stretch all the way up the Nile to Aswan, three hundred miles to the south. To the west, Manshiyat Nasir's boundary is determined by the filtration area into which all of Cairo's sewage lines pour. To the north is the major thoroughfare of Umar ibn Abd al-Aziz, and immediately to the south sits the sacred space on which Gamal Abd al-Nasir stood when he made his historic gesture. It is basically one modest street, the greatest significance of which is that it is the battlefield for a permanent war between the sewage administration and the bureau of road-works. From it branch little side streets bearing nonconsecutive numbers (it isn't clear why). At the beginning of the street you are met by the Star of Helwan Café. There are cafés all up and down the street, but they are frequented by outsiders. The reigning belief in the neighborhood is that respectable workers don't spend their time sitting in cafés.

The Newtown. It's a mongrel place, part village and part unplanned city fringe, destination of squatters and incomers, although, thanks to the wave of Gamal Abd al-Nasir's hand, it has a definite class identity. And perhaps by virtue of that very same gesture, the Manshiyat's residents are well placed to look down their noses at the populace of adjacent neighborhoods. Although they have rebelled against the tin shacks they threw up immediately after the historic hand flick—rebelled and moved into real houses—they remain loyal to their villages, those faraway farming villages that they never, ever visit, yet the memories of which give them a sense of security and protect them from the betrayals of time and the bosses at the factory. If you ask a resident where he lives, he will respond proudly with the name of a tiny village in some governorate, and if you have any inclination to listen he will favor you with a detailed telling of the dramatic circumstances that forced him to leave it. And so they are always on watch for the day in which they will leave the Newtown behind and return to their villages, like the soldier impatiently anticipating his next leave or the emigrant longing permanently for his own people.

10

The Justice is a President of Court from Beni Sweif: he's from the same town as Prof Ramadan's Beauty Queen. He met Gamal by chance at a hash soiree hosted by an officer in Maadi. The mutual and profound contemplation that their state of high exhilaration allowed meant that each took the measure of the other's talents and reckoned how best to take brilliant advantage of him. Gamal had the benefit of initiative—"Whoa, there, a lighter hand, Pasha!" The Justice had been a little intemperate in the size of the chunk he'd rolled into his cigarette. Now he was embarrassed.

"Don't mind me, sorry, it's just . . . I haven't had a good lungful for days."

"No, no, Pasha! That's not what I meant, how could I!" and Gamal doubled over laughing, his words fading, obliging his companion to draw closer.

"So then what *did* you mean?"

"I meant . . . I meant, in court, Pasha! People are so beaten down and anyway, everyone will get what's coming to him in the end."

Naturally the Justice considered Gamal's allusion a major in-sult to his already scuffed honor. He rounded on the head of the household—how could he have brought him into the company of such filthy types?—and then stalked out in a fury. The following evening his voice snaked out of Gamal's cell phone, ready to conclude an Accord with All Fine Points agreed on.

The Justice and the accused men over whose case he would preside were implacable adversaries; the two sides were looking for a brief truce permitting them some sort of mutually agreeable situation. He could be brought around with money, while they would be more than satisfied with an acquittal or even a lighter sentence (since everything has its price). Gamal was merely a go-between. A neutral space and a secure one perfectly suited for a smooth and uncomplicated swap based on each party's interests. Gamal combined in his person the attributes of delinquency, justice, and risk that enabled him to weigh the scales of justice perfectly, balancing the issues that had forced each party into this face-to-face situation.

In court, the process ran its course. Gamal had to sit in on the trial sessions for major cases that (the justice let him know) would end in nothing less than death sentences or, at best, life. Immediately before the scheduled sentencing, Gamal would offer his services to the family of the accused as an ordinary lawyer: " 'Course, I don't hafta tell *you* folks . . . the case is a tough one, very complex, but don't worry. . . . Relax, the big guy's an old friend of ours, *Inshaallah* it'll work out at about five years, maybe he'll be cleared, who knows, everything has its own accounting." He'd provide them with a gilt-edged card: "In the apartme—I mean, in the office we can talk without any hassles."

It wasn't long, though, before Gamal disappeared from the trial sessions altogether. He had opened a court in his apartment, a real trial court where the cases were out in the open, rulings came down starting in the very first session, and no one was weighed down by the heavy complications of The Law. This court was the refuge of the accused whose cases were to be argued in the Justice's chamber. They would confess the minutest details before Gamal, who listened, as a judge—a true judge, ruling fairly, taking into account the magnitude of the crime and the circumstances of the guilty defendant (for it appears that people have opportunities to mount justice in all circumstances). Moreover, the probable fine was known to all sides in the game. In a case of smuggling hashish involving a capable major trader, penalties began at one hundred thousand pounds, with a quarter of finest hashish thrown in as an involuntary contribution to the after-trial party in celebration of his innocence, by God's leave. But a case of goods distribution involving some poor young sod would go at most to five thousand pounds, and the guy to whom he was apprenticed would pay it. As for murder—it depended on the category. Killing a woman in normal circumstances, ten thousand pounds, but if she had cheated on her husband, three thousand only. For killing a man who was spineless, even if he had stolen something, a quarter sufficed. The income was divided by the judge, on principles of justice. One share to the dame who presided over his apartment and another to cover the expenses of hosting the customers, while the rest went, untouched, into the pocket of the Justice: "By God don't let anyone into this business—we're the only go-betweens—from your hand to mine, that's all the hands we need."

The Justice was quick to stand by the family in emergencies, without expecting any compensation, as if interceding to get Amer off the hook on the many occasions in which he had been caught red-handed smoking bango right out in the street, before the matter could get as far as the public prosecutor's office. Or facilitating Sayf's rapid admission to the mental hospital without going through the usual examination. Or being prepared to fabricate a terrorism case for Shaykh Hasan. Counting on the strength of his relationship with the Justice, Abu Hanan (Gamal's uncle on his mother's side) took a gamble and put his life's savings into a shipment of hashish. When the undercover antinarcotics force seized it—in his possession—the Justice came forward and had the case transferred to his chambers. He was intending to issue an acquittal but no sooner did he actually see Abu Hanan there inside the bars of the cage than the guy took on the look of one of his ordinary customers: a professional criminal who according to the wheels of justice must pay a fine. Doubled.

With his loathing for narcotics dealers, the Justice finds money a fitting punishment for them: if they're dealing for the sake of money, after all, then fairness dictates that we prohibit them from having it. In their case imprisonment doesn't work. In fact, inside prison they pick up their business activities, but with more security than before. Therefore, the Justice proposed an appropriate amendment to the antinarcotics law in an article he published in one of the newspapers. When this unleashed a violent campaign launched against him by the men of justice, he was convinced that there was nothing for it but to apply his amendment himself.

He informed Gamal. "We've transferred Old Lucky to your jurisdiction, old fella!" and Gamal assumed he was feeling greedy for praise and wanting to be thanked for his efforts on behalf of the uncle. So Gamal was effusive. "God preserve you, Pasha, where would we all be without you?!"

The Justice sensed that he had to offer some clarification. "*At least* a quarter million pounds—this guy wouldn't escape with less than life."

"Quarter million! The guy's cleaned out. No need to make a

fuss over details with him, after all he's one of us, families stick together, good times and bad."

"No, no—that's not the point here! This is a case, a real one.
He either pays or he gets put in the clink."

So Gamal found himself in a real mess. He had to confess to
the Justice that he'd made a deal with his uncle—"innocent" if
he'd renounce that debt, the cost of the hash Gamal had taken
back in the days when they were in business.

"Fine. Then *you* come up with it."

"Pasha, you know we got no extra here, what comes in goes
out."

The other one stood his ground. A fine was a fine. In court,
he showed no hesitation. He sentenced Abu Hanan to life.

11

Sayf came home from the loony bin. Came back in possession of a mind guaranteed by the government: he had an official certificate of witness stamped with the signatures of some movers and shakers among physicians. Embossed at the foot of the page, to guard against any doubt, was the official Eagle of the Republic. Sayf pulled this document from his pocket and waved it around like a weapon in the face of an enemy. He handed it to Prof Ramadan with an impertinent gesture that was a clear stand-in for a tongue-lashing. "Read . . . read and recite, so the bastards will shut up."

The Ustadh wiped his glasses and began to examine the documentary evidence on Sayf's brain with the usual care of someone rifling through the contents of a person's head in front of a ready crowd. For people had gathered around Abu Gamal's chair in front of the house. It was a testimony acutely embarrassing to all—the crowd, Abu Gamal, and even the Prof himself. Who, after all, holds definitive proof of the soundness of his own mind equivalent to the certificate he was turning over in his hands right now? . . . On the reverse of the certificate appeared more glad tidings, borne in a letter addressed, unofficially, to Abu Gamal and bearing the signature of a psychiatrist. Though terse, it was conclusive. The Prof read it aloud in a tone of voice that captured the splendor of its language. "Successful treatment of the above-named individual resides not in the hospital but rather in the stable family. If your concern is as we anticipate . . . marry him off . . . marry him off immediately."

Um Gamal let out with a series of ululations that was as loud and as long as she could manage. "Congratulations, Sayf! *Congratulations*, son!" And then she burst out sobbing, the picture of a defendant who has just gotten a pronouncement of innocence after having been falsely accused. Since Gamal could find no way to wriggle out of this situation, he threatened to leave for good. "So now that son of a bitch pansy'll be lying on his back right in this house!" Abd al-Halim, on the other hand, was in a receptive state of mind and thinking about Nada. "Nothing unusual in this, even the president of Ameerka doesn't get anywhere unless he makes the homos happy. And if its marriage we're talking about, well, the bride is all decked out already, or . . . whaddaya think, Prof?"

The Prof had something else on his mind. A literary subject. A poem in which he goads the populace to carry documents specifying the ranking of their brains and—based on that—delineating appropriate modes of interaction. Instead of identity cards that make no distinction between the sane and the mad.

Nada—"Morning Dew"—had been waiting for Sayf like a drowning person hoping for a length of straw as a means of rescue. She knew, that is, that her circumstances wouldn't extend to marriage outside the context of family solidarity. And Sayf was the only one of her uncle's sons who hadn't married yet. Moreover, for his sake she had been sacrificing forty pounds every six months to renew the potency of the love amulet a sorcerer from

Maasara had written five years before, telling her to put it at a spot near the heart. From that day on the amulet never left her brassiere.

She was just short enough to be a perfect match for Sayf. She suffered from a skinniness that was less a result of wasting away from unrequited passion than an indicator of poor nutrition (or none at all). She loved to sing. To be more precise, Nada was a Singer-with-a-capital-S whose performances focused on a single song whose opening lyrics raised an existential question that was tough to crack: "Me—who am I? M-e-e, who am I? M-e-e-e-e . . . who am I?" Because she knew herself very well, however, she was able to give further details:

> I'm the one with wounds all over
> For so long hurt, without a lover
> Sapped by time as you can see,
> And no one is in love with me.
> When I moan *"Aaaah"*
> People say *"Allaaah!"*
> I'm the one of grief unending,
> Whose blissful day is ever pending,
> I'm the one who lives alone
> But for my sorrows I'm on my own . . .

. . . Older than Sayf by about five years, Nada had the face of a little girl whose mom remarried and whose dad then abandoned her to the keeping of his only brother, Abu Gamal. On the night of her wedding to Sayf, she laughed for perhaps the first time in her life. She laughed with an earnest constancy and a cackle that had a significant and dual impact: first, it messed up the makeup lines on her face; the stripe of kohl overspilled into something resembling a trench until it mixed with the red undulating across her lips. Second, that guffaw, so unanticipated from a bride who was meant to be diffidence itself, determined from the start the future of her relationship with the family of this house—first and foremost among them Um Gamal.

She crossed the threshold into the stairwell apartment that faced the Doctoress's door holding Sayf's hand. She was in a state of confusion, regarded and evaluated by all not as a bride but as a cure for insanity, a bitter and useless pill. She knew, though, that the solution was in her hands. Marriage is a blessing that had fallen to her unexpectedly from the heavens, and all that remained to be done was to prove her aptitude. She sacrificed and dedicated herself and with the completion of the first, celebratory forty days of marriage, her efforts bore fruit . . . the signs of pregnancy made themselves known.

"Omigod, Nada's pregnant! Fine, then, but where did that come from?"

12

"So, you're living next to Koftes, aren't you?"

Taking me unawares with this bit of information, Abu Gamal chose a tone of voice appropriate to someone who has rendered an honorable service. Although I did my best to appear annoyed and upset, in fact I all but gave him a kiss. For having Koftes as a neighbor in this house specifically as good as guaranteed some degree of security and a natural, normal life inside your apartment. You could talk to yourself and laugh without any embarrassment, you could turn up the volume on the radio louder than necessary and dance if you felt like it, and have your friends over just to exchange the latest shades of gossip and all of you could hoot as noisily as you wanted while you consumed forbidden substances. More important than any of this, having Koftes there meant I could finally enjoy the sensation of pitying someone else.

Pity. The resort of the slothful. Pity allows you to come to terms with the disasters in your own life by dwelling on the catastrophes of others. Pity cons you into believing that you are a truly generous person. That you are noble and courageous, with nothing to lose but a sympathetic gaze that you part with easily and deliver sincerely. Pity is the sign of power. The sign of that generous impulse to give unto others that left me when I left the Bedouin, for everyone else was always stronger and I was always the one cut out for shows of grief and likely even some tears.

According to the dictionary, the word *koftes* approximates the English "Copt" or "Copts" or the French "Coopti," and they all mean what we call in Arabic *qibti* in everyday speech *ibti* or in other words someone of the Coptic religion or a person from ancient Egypt. When applied to Adil, however, it meant something else, something beyond an insult. Hearing it, he would erupt as if he had just gotten an invisible bite from a snake. And because our ears are highly trained at picking up whatever wounds us, he was erupting constantly.

There are moments in everyone's life that live forever. Moments that one always returns to in one's memory, again and again, that one relies on for help in constructing one's role in life. Moments akin to the fleeting smile of a girl, or the wrinkles in a face you saw only once in your life but it remains clear in your mind. These moments contradict each other, and some are more important than others, but they fix the rhythm of our deeds and harmonize our outlooks on life.

Adil—"Man of Just Mind"—is from the city of Sohag, and so he and Shaykh Hasan hail from the same place. In Sohag, something simple happened to him that might have passed quietly into the fog of forgotten memories just as other events did. Contrary to reasonable expectation, though, it embedded itself in his memory—implanted itself and swelled with the passage of time. Adil recalls its details fully. Or, to be more exact, whenever he does anything the memory returns, not because he yearns for childhood's escapades but rather in anticipation of having to foil the event's recurrence. When we're struck suddenly with some disaster that we can't extricate ourselves from, we tend to dwell feverishly on every detail of it, perhaps to accustom ourselves to its painful outcome.

Adil was fifteen at the time, adept at shimmying up date palms and an able strategist when it came to seizing fruit-laden territory. Like any boy, he was part of an inseparable gang. They were on one of their usual expeditions, seeking fun and naughtiness, when they got very thirsty. But they were out in the fields, tangled up in the undergrowth, and there was nothing around but the shaykh's hut. It was a tiny, cramped prayer shelter that Shaykh Atuwwa had had built smack in the middle of the fields, in his eagerness to lay down the law for peasants too lazy to perform God's prayers on the excuse that the mosque was so far away, and also his zeal about preserving and protecting his religious standing now that new generations of shaykhs were at the helm in the village mosque. Adil wasn't comfortable with the idea of drinking water from the jug in Shaykh Atuwwa's *zawiya,* especially as Adil even avoided going anywhere near that place. Yet, swayed by thirst, the midday heat, and his father's warnings that he would pick up bilharzia[1] if he so much as stepped into the irrigation canals, Adil followed the gang.

The shaykh was taking his rest at the prayer shelter's door, his head bared of the usual turban cloth and a rather large water jug swinging just overhead. The shaykh had had to attach this *qulla*

1. Bilharzia, also called schistosomiasis, is a disease caused by parasitic worms; it is widespread in much of the semitropical and tropical world. Infection occurs when the skin comes into contact with contaminated water in which snails carrying *Schistosoma* eggs live; the effects range from severe nausea to blindness.

by a rope to the ceiling and to sleep directly beneath it; otherwise, by now it would have met the same fate as its sisters, stolen
one after the other. The qulla was close enough to the ground to
be within reach, but anyone who wanted to drink from it was
obliged to make a very gingerly and polite approach. You had to
lift the *qulla* very carefully about a meter high until it was level
with your mouth, but without disturbing the hallowed head of
the shaykh, from whose feet—dirty of course—it was separated
only by an embarrassingly small margin.

The boys knew the whole procedure well, naturally. They
crept close one by one, and their mouths successfully gave the
mouth of the jug a series of passionate kisses, until Adil's turn
came. He was well behind the others and hurried up in a state of
disarray, raised the qulla to his mouth, and awaited the pleasure of
a fresh, clear waterfall. The only problem was that the sleeping
Shaykh Atuwwa seems to have sensed impending danger, for he
suddenly shot upward, causing Adil to lose his control over the
heavy jug. It swung directly across the crown of the shaykh's head
as that head was moving toward it, with the intention of rescuing
it from the boys. It shattered and blood gushed out like a foun-
tain, though a somewhat sluggish one. The shaykh's body thud-
ded to the ground with what sounded and felt like an
earthquake. Terrified, the boys whirled round to face Adil. It was
at that moment that they discovered their friend to be in fact an
enemy. Naturally, he had to bear the full brunt of a young and
vigorous revolution. The act of pounding his body to a pulp gave
them a perfect symbolic idiom through which to express their
holy struggle as they atoned for the crime of having considered
him a friend. And then, drinking his blood offered the best of
outlets for the overwhelming emotions of a whole village of

peasants, as they proclaimed an abiding faith whose existence the shaykh had always doubted.

🌀 It's always easier to tell the truth than to fabricate a first-rate lie. I have worn myself out imagining, or more precisely composing, a violent dramatic scenario that would justify to the reader, or at least get across, the tense relationship between Adil and the word *koftes*. I have struggled to give historical depth to his loathing for the word. But it is easier, in the end, just to relate the truth of the matter. To say that Shaykh Atuwwa didn't actually jump up, his head wasn't really crushed, and I'm certain that he wasn't even particularly bothered by the appearance of Adil at his *zawiya*. That he let Adil drink as all the other boys had, without anything more than a quick glance, a fleeting glance that Adil expected and which had the fate of sticking forever in his mind though at that moment he simply faced it with silence. Utter silence. In such circumstances, silence is expressive of two contradictory possibilities: either fear or deliberately keeping very still in preparation for a big and eventful leap. But Adil's silence is always a goal all in itself, a manifestation of silence's power to overwhelm, to suggest nothing other than the awesome presence of the gods keeping watch. Or, for Adil, silence signals a threshold moment in preparation for the full expression of his powers, which he articulates by bursting into sobs. Adil's weeping has a hard edge that seems a little off for a person who has been humiliated, indeed a person whose display of tears is meant as an in-your-face insult, in this case to Shaykh Atuwwa. Humiliation, like all of those emotions we try to put a name to, is relative and its force depends normally on the intentions of the person who is offering the insult. Sometimes we convey more meaning when

we humiliate someone by exaggerating our own weaknesses—
by showing ourselves as utterly crushed. Especially if that person
knows we can do nothing else.

Adil is about thirty years old now, and what you'll notice in
his face is a mustache resembling the handlebars of a little kid's
bike. He has the eyes of a perennial insomniac. He's moderately
tall, or let's just say that his body overall is about what a good
swimmer would want. His level of academic achievement is
pretty hard to make out: we'll hear "Institute of Technology and
Commerce" one time and "secondary school diploma exam" on
some other occasion. Even if his own sense of achievement leaves
him feeling a bit ashamed, because his uncle's university-
educated daughter refused to marry him, he is to be considered—in either of the two cases—one of the distinguished
academic degree-holders in the likes of such a house as ours, and
perhaps throughout the length and breadth of Manshiyat Nasir.
He is a man of few words: to be more precise about it, he never
talks at all. Perhaps if he had acquired the skill of eloquent speech
he would have described his situation more profoundly than did
that English lady encountered by the psychologist Robert Burton in his famous work *Anatomy of Melancholy* when she described not being able to breathe outside of her own home, and
not being able to stand on her own two shaking legs, and so, she
said, she never left home. It happened gradually at first, she said;
in a crowd, she said, "I couldn't breathe, or I felt afraid, and if I
went out to get something and found the shop crowded I would
leave right away. If I took a bus, I always wanted to get where I
was going as fast as possible . . . all of these things happened gradually at first, but they got worse. . . . I cried. I was always crying."
(So it's a book from the seventeenth century. Same idea, buses or
no buses.)

Adil is a clever guy, blessed with the caution of a person faced with having to eliminate potential hazards all too often. Simply on the basis of his experience and expertise in this area he could have gotten on just fine, keeping to himself and keeping from mixing with the inhabitants at No. 36. But because he was so uncertain of being worthy of their confidence, together with his inflated respect for the worth of confidence itself, living quietly among us was out of the question. *The more convinced we are of the difficulty of obtaining some thing, the greater grows its worth in our eyes.* Here was a thought that Gamal wrote down, once.

Adil exists in a state of permanent fear. It may well be that those who live in fear cannot be free, or perhaps they're never able to take firm decisions and act. But there's no denying that these folks are the ablest of anyone at discovering what their own strong points are in the eyes of those around them. Adil's neighbors truly feared his presence—you know how you act when you don't know someone, how you take care to conceal details of what you do every day? You don't necessarily suspect that person of deliberately concealing some hidden power. But there's an anxiety that gnaws at you when you feel you have to be on guard against someone you know is weak but you can't be sure what naughtiness he might be capable of. Adil fought back against this fear by constantly going too far out of his way, sacrificing his comfort for the sake of making his neighbors comfortable. Not simply to gain their confidence but also to prove to himself that he was not that alien person who merits suspicion, who gives you the creeps and makes you constitutionally cautious.

He followed Abu Gamal closely. Stuck with him like his shadow. This wasn't a question of simple parasitism; after all, it was a fruitful attachment. Abu Gamal always had something nearby that he wanted repaired: the door to the chicken coop, the spigot in the stairwell, the ceiling fan or the drain. Not only was Adil at his beck and call. Adil, in fact, was skilled in a number of technical fields: carpentry, painting and decorating, plumbing, electricity. He fixed everything with great dedication and nobility. At first, Abu Gamal's reaction was to take it all as a down payment on a friendship that was only to be expected from this new resident. As the days went on, though, the older man began to look upon Adil's constant self-renunciation as no more and no less than father-right—that right he'd been deprived of when he was afflicted with disobedient offspring, a right due him as a man of a certain age who coveted the respectful gaze of others.

Adil didn't work. Or, let's just say that he didn't last where work was concerned. And so, at 8 a.m., Abu Gamal would wake him up, and after they partook communally of Um Gamal's breakfast the daily round of work commenced. They'd look into the state of the hut that housed the chickens, continue with a quick tour around the building's utilities, and round out the day by cleaning and sprinkling the strategic stretch in front of the house. Then Abu Gamal would settle himself into his chair and begin telling his life story to Adil, who sat at his feet. This wasn't the life story that everyone in the vicinity already knew, but rather a tale of escapades that Abu Gamal was hoping everyone would hear.

"Mind, now, boy. . . . See here, Adil, my old man he was a nervy one. Used to weld the door shut after evening prayer every night and didn't open up until the dawn call. He kept us going like a clock and anyone who was going to be late slept out if he knew what was good for him. Once the old guy popped in suddenly when we were smoking, and we ate the cigs." Abu Gamal let out a shriek of laughter and Adil tried his best to respond in kind. "Know what, I put out that butt and swallowed it, believe it, by God to this day I remember its taste in my mouth, but hey we all grew up men, from when I was seven years old I drove those manure donkeys hard, and gathered cotton and did . . . and every penny I worked for he swallowed, and when I turned seventeen he up and married me to Um Gamal, now that was a gal from a family that got right respect, but my pop, everyone knew his name around the place."

As Abu Gamal went on, Adil was otherwise occupied. He was mounting a search in his own head for some examples of heroism that could make him proud of his own father. Not to relate them to Abu Gamal, but to work up a little internal esprit de corps with the older man's tales. Fawzi had been the village's only carpenter. Windows, doors, hoes and axes, threshers, waterwheels—all were the work of his hands, and all bore some resemblance to him. To go further, and due to Fawzi, these works all served as material evidence of the potential for realizing socialism and equality in Egyptian village society.

The village houses had outside doors composed of a single large panel. Two-thirds of the way up, an iron hand closed powerfully around an iron ball, ready to knock on the metal plate affixed to the wooden door. Precisely halfway down were two pieces of wood carved in the shape of a virgin girl's rising breasts. On the inside was fixed a pair of big hinges and a bolt with a strong resemblance to a sword that had known some courageous combat.

Fawzi enjoyed the utter confidence of his customers. He belonged to that dying class of people who believed that perfection was a goal in itself, apart from customer satisfaction. He had a

personal relationship going with those pieces of wood based on
the understanding that they would be the only traces remaining
of him after he had passed away. At one point, he took on the job
of repairing the village mosque's roof, which was basically a few
wooden beams laid over with boards. With the years, one of the
beams had split down the middle and now it needed to be taken
out and replaced. The task wasn't as easy as it appeared; the split
beam was the supporting one, the chief beam, the core on which
the entire mosque roof depended. Fawzi's strategy was founded
on a scheme for fortifying the roof first. He would erect several
solidly attached pillars before removing the split beam. And it all
happened exactly as he had planned: the supporting columns,
once in place, appeared capable of bearing the roof's weight for
eternity.

🦋 Fawzi stood atop the roof. The men brought a double ladder
over and rested it at the head of the broken beam, which they
began drawing out with a rope. Slowly at first, it obeyed them,
and then the rest of it slipped out smoothly and easily without
causing any rupture in the roof.

Adil was standing below, observing—as were others of the
village—his father's wisdom, though he was anticipating some
sort of an Event that would interrupt the process. Meanwhile,
Fawzi was moving along the roof with complete confidence and
easy agility, immune to all worry except the possibility that some
hitch in his plan would suddenly come to light. True, the
mosque roof was the product of his own hands and he knew its
strong points and its weaknesses intimately. But Fawzi was prone
to fear that his projects would not be carried out with the necessary precision, the care he hoped for and counted on from oth-

ers. To repair a door or window or even a village dining table barely a foot off the ground was to face a critical test; the trial posed by an entire mosque roof was beyond imagining.

As usual, Fawzi passed the test beautifully and the new beam went into the space left by the old one exactly as he had planned. He walked about on the roof to test it. For added assurance, he began stamping on it as if compressing a sack of raw cotton. The roof's firmness was satisfying, but apparently he stamped a little too vigorously, a little more heavily than the beam could bear, and suddenly the whole roof collapsed. The new beam broke, then the one next to it and the one next to that all at once, and the mosque was suddenly an awesome heap of wood debris, with Fawzi brought down right smack in the middle.

From all sides people rushed forward into the wreckage. They were able to pull him out, but only with great difficulty. Despite the wounds and broken bones he was smiling, though perhaps a bit shamefaced.

Adil barely leaves the house. He's at everyone's service, yet with unbelievable skill he convinces them repeatedly that he is not a servant but rather a man of dignity worthy to receive their trust and respect. And Abu Gamal has come to consider him a son. His true and real son. The son for whom he has longed.

Abu Gamal hasn't stinted on anything when it comes to Adil: food, drink, blankets according to the winter chill's dictates—and every evening a new chapter in the story. "If you get to the bottom of it, this Manshiya really ought to be written in my name. I'd only been in the factory one single month the day Gamal Abd al-Nasir showed his face. The foreman just about died right there, he was so scared, and I went and stood up to him like a true lion and gave him a real mouthful, right out loud.

"Pasha, we got no place to sleep in. Can't find us a spot any-where." And so then he did it, he pointed right at Manshiya, it was just waste ground then, that's right, Allah! Empty land. And if you don't believe me, pictures don't lie," and Abu Gamal points to a dented photo in which he stands tall as the hand of the Leader and Commander rests on the back of his neck, behind them an empty space that looks like an unused dump.

Adil gives it an intent look, as always, but takes care (as al-ways) not to gawp—as much as he can avoid it, anyway—at the bottom of the picture where you can see Abu Gamal's bare feet. And then Abu Gamal snatches it away from him. "Don't get your head going about it!—back in those days, work was right work."

Adil met Amer by chance. For a long time, Adil barely knew what Amer looked like, since Amer slept all day and began his evening with his quality smoke before setting out with the guys in search of a nicely secure conduit for obtaining some bango. More to the point, Adil stuck close by Abu Gamal while Amer avoided coming in sight of his father's face as much as he possibly could.

In a sense, Amer was apart from it all. He didn't play any role to speak of in the household. Abu Gamal never mentioned him in his tales except as incontrovertible proof of the new genera-tion's corruption, and it was perhaps exactly this that gave Adil to anticipate his friendship, indeed made Adil burn to see him. He always had his suspicions about Abu Gamal's estimation of things.

When Amer came home at dawn one day, arriving stoned out of his head as usual, he overestimated the number of floors he had to climb to reach his apartment two floors above. He went up an extra story and stopped in front of Adil's apartment. When all his exertions could produce was a bent and twisted key, he began shoving at the door violently, thinking that Zannuba had locked it from inside as she often did. He was taken by surprise: it was Adil who stood in the open doorway in something of a panic. "Sorry, brother. Is Zannuba here?"

"Zannuba? . . . Zannuba who?"

"Uuuh. So, I got the apartment wrong." And he leaned on the balustrade and began staring into the stairwell. "So what floor are we on."

"Third."

"Aha—and I was just saying to myself, why's the apartment so far to get to this time. Goodnight, sleep well, then." Amer leered straight into Adil's startled face. "Hey, don't worry about it, so a guy gets a little happy now and then." He staggered down the stairs.

The next evening Adil waited for him in front of the house. Amer was uncomfortable and hesitant. Adil tried to get him to realize there was no cause for embarrassment and that it was all very simple. A word from here, another from there, and the two of them were pretty well acquainted. Amer expressed his pleasure on that score by inviting Adil to a convivial early-morning session. Adil turned down the invitation, making his excuses.

Adil loves jokes and banter. He always gets the punch line. And Amer has a crying need for a pal who can appreciate his puns when they're having a high time. It was only a matter of days before Adil became one of the bango gang.

The chummier I have tried to get with Adil's character, the faster and farther he has pulled away. Even though I haven't attempted to butt in on his relationship with Amer, and before that with Abu Gamal—except to help him out—the two of them have continually popped up in my face, with the consequence that he stays in the shadow.

Maybe it was because his character was deeper than was my capacity to understand it, maybe it was that I did not know him well the whole time I lived in this building. As far as I was concerned, he was simply a predictably steady and easy neighbor, and the one time I saw him face to face was actually a little embarrassing. One evening, sensing movement in front of the door to my apartment, I put my ear to the keyhole. I heard nothing, so I opened the door suddenly, and there was Adil, scurrying back into his apartment and slamming the door in my face. To this day I don't know what he was doing at the door to my apartment, or why he displayed obvious fear merely at the sight of me.

"Come on. *Yallah,* hurry up, yours for mine, might be that our Lord'll pave the way" . . . said Amer to Adil. This was an anticipated culmination to an idea they had been turning over in their heads for some time. "You know, it's a real plan, really is." "Okay, man, I can promise you my gang . . . bling by the truckload, might build an entire mosque. You make sure of your group."

"Make sure of them?"

"Make sure of 'em, come on, those fellows could make you boss in the world's toughest town."

They were sitting in Amer's apartment waiting for the rest of the gang to return from their after-dark mission. Amer was engrossed in rolling the last cigarette as if party to a sacred and prescribed ritual. Rolling, for him, was a goal in itself; he would twirl the finished product before his eyes with an uncommon pleasure. And then he'd pass it to Adil whose valiant exertions to avert his glance from Zannuba's posterior were almost successful. And they were gone in their dreams. Adil saw himself borne along on various shoulders, held high above the crowd, his beard now long. Amer saw himself straying in confusion through strange climes, no doubt the home place he had chosen.

Adil and Amer are unemployed; or let's just say that they don't give high priority to committing themselves to any specific job. Abu Gamal interceded on behalf of each and got them work in the textile factory. But they bid the factory farewell each in a manner that surely embarrassed Abu Gamal. Amer's approach was to empty out all the contents of the first truck that fell into his hands—right down to and including the motor. Adil found that a personal work stoppage was the ideal way to be fired from the factory without the intervention of any complicating factors.

13

I was on my balcony and Sayf stood next to me. Zannuba was immediately below us. She was exhibiting her talents for the Beauty Queen of Beni Sweif. As usual, she was in competition with the Beauty Queen for the eyes of her husband, but not with the aim of pursuing an honorable competition, as this appeared to be rivalry with the aim of offering service or an expression from one rival of her irritation at the failings of her antagonist. "Hey sister, give it a little more horsepower! The man's a live one!"

She knew our ears were greedy to pick up whatever she had to say, and that delighted her. Zannuba is consistently intent on announcing how pitiful she finds the attempts of Prof Ramadan. She doesn't reject his efforts. She just wants to make sure it is obvious to everyone that this looks-and-smiles strategy is not the right way to go about it when it comes to the likes of her.

Zannuba wasn't pretty in the commonly accepted sense. But she could lay claim to a divinely appointed capacity for seduction; to put it differently, it was easy for her to work up the God-given sexual aptitudes of anyone and everyone in sight. What got me going, personally, was a thin black glistening line—it was *always* thin, black and glistening—that lay taut along her left shoulder. This was the strap that supported her chest, or her breast, or . . . I can't find an appropriate term at this point. It seems that language itself has failed to yield an expression that would do justice to the splendor of this thing that is held in suspension by a glistening thin strip. This dearth of appropriate language may be due to the discomfiture of the ancient Arabs, or perhaps it's because silence is the best strategy when you're working to bag a prey . . .

Zannuba's neckline droops eternally. From my position on the balcony I can see the thin strip as it passes the midpoint between her neck and the highest altitude on the slope of her shoulder. To the rear it continues down her back, and when she leans across to the Ustadh's balcony railing—and usually she does—I'll see one plane of the murky region into which the front half of that strip plunges. A thin black glistening thread, whose twin I ripped off a shirt belonging to my wife, unrolled it in front of me, and began stroking gently. An ordinary satin strip, but when it settles itself into its place over Zannuba's shoulder, it's a different order of being.

Sayf is a sly character. He knew—from experience, naturally—what I wanted. He knew exactly what I wanted. "You want her," he stated with no doubt in his voice, and that messed me up, left me looking like a guy who's caught red-handed in an extremely compromising situation. I tried to cover myself by claiming I didn't catch his meaning. "Excuse me?" But my response was awkwardly contrived somewhere between denial and confirmation, which just made it easier for him to jump immediately to his ultimate meaning. "To get on top of her, that is." Now the wise course was to keep entirely quiet, while he launched into the minutiae of his nighttime scheme, which would put me within reach of Zannuba.

"See, nothing to it. You'll put out the lights in your apartment, and the light on the stairs, and then you have the door open just a little bit, and you're standing behind it, okay? When Zannuba comes in you close it real fast—and the rest is up to you. You just watch out you don't cause us a scandal, and for my part, I'll guarantee the house doesn't find out."

I didn't ask him, of course, what position Zannuba was taking on all of this, or what devilish method he had in mind to convince her of the plan. His confidence was evidence enough of his expertise and a sure indication that she was in his pocket and that the two of them had already gotten a few similar schemes off the ground without a hitch.

That evening I followed his instructions to the letter. I took care of whatever lights were on in my apartment, and then I turned out the light in the stairwell. I'd put some hard effort into making sure the key that turned the stairwell light on and off was in my possession: it had to do with my insatiable need to exert some kind of domestic authority. I positioned the door so it was carefully angled open. I waited. I was calm, since as far as I was concerned the whole thing was a game that I found entertaining.

But now it was crossing over into something serious, for I could actually see Zannuba at the landing closest to my door. She was apprehensive, or confused, wrapped in something I couldn't make out, maybe a black *milaya* for outside wear, maybe a blanket. I had a sense of danger but it vanished when pitted against the skill the two of them had about slipping into my apartment exactly as the plan's clauses had laid out.

It was certain that everything was happening in just the way it was supposed to and that Sayf would fulfill his role consummately, guaranteeing the safety of the site until we were finished. I closed the door firmly and hurled myself onto her, and she pushed me away, as might be expected, slipped out of my grasp, and slid onto the bed, with me leaping after her. After a little interval in which I lost my balance and knocked into things, I successfully established my authority. I cornered her, though from behind. That didn't slow me down, since I don't have any strong feelings one way or the other on the whole issue of positions, and perhaps this was the position that best suited her. It was pitch-black around us, but never mind, no difficulty there since in circumstances like these, blindness is a blessing. But no sooner did I get a good, deep breath of air than the suspicion seized me that it was really Sayf and that the object spreading gloriously in front of me was his butt, so I slowed down, or rather, I came to a stop. It was a truly embarrassing situation to be in, and for a moment I lost my powers of distinction. I recalled with a sort of awe Yusuf Idris's blind man in his short story "House of Flesh." There was no possibility of retreat, no escape from completing the matter at hand in accordance with the plan's precisely laid out procedures.

On the next occasion all embarrassment would evaporate. And with experience I would grow capable of making necessary distinctions. An illusion that he was Zannuba would take up its place as a translucent drape that allowed us to continue the game with rare and perfect skill, and likewise to enjoy its recurrences in our conversation, like any two friends taking delight—as most folks do—in recounting and remembering the details of their adventures together. What was reported wasn't what actually took place but rather what could be prettified in memory. It is so very pleasant to tell an event, or a story, to a person who already knows it in detail. This spares you the hard work of remembering a lot of the obvious and trivial bits of it so that you can get right to the heart of the matter, relying on your storytelling talents. The beauty of an episode is never appreciated as it's happening, but it appears in all its glory when re-created in the balconies of memory by means of a great narrative for a friend you trust. So, for example . . . the beauty of meeting a beloved is something you can't take pleasure in the moment it happens, really, but rather once you've rid yourself of the eyes of the moralists and the very presence of that lover and you shut yourself away with a good friend in front of whom you reenact the scene of encounter exactly as you wish, erasing the flaws that weighed down the scene and hampered its graceful movement as it was happening, and then you add what seems like it should have happened but didn't, and you alter the pace and rhythm as you wish, so that indeed the beloved's gorgeous looks and spirit and extent of desire for you become like soft plasticine over the flame of your highly skilled and seriously artistic memory, and you immerse yourself in the fog of a happiness that will never lift.

I didn't face any difficulties at all in describing the details of my adventures with Zannuba to Sayf. After all, I was tackling the role of someone I knew pretty well. "Can you believe it, today we could've easily fallen right off the bed, unhuh, by God, Zannuba was trembling so hard I was afraid she'd collapse right in my apartment—what a scandal we'd have on our hands then!"

Sayf's role was to work his imagination sufficiently to come up with descriptions that were in line with his prowess as guard and master architect of the whole operation while remaining appropriate to Zannuba's delicacy. "I was barely keeping my eyes open, keeping watch up there, Pop wouldn't settle down, every couple minutes he's crawling up the damn chicken shed, and meanwhile you've got it where you want it, you're going at it and your damn thing won't quit."

14

*Hell is when you stand on the exact midpoint
    between two opposing things.
Between wealth and poverty.
Between success and failure.
Between realizing your goal and retreating from it.
Between talent and illusion.*

Gamal had ambitions to write an extended composition on the Professor, but this passage was as far as he got.

Prof Ramadan was one of those people who wallow in their easily summoned feelings of shame and who have great respect for shadowy matters such as honor and pride. He loved Zannuba passionately, loved her truly and wasted many long nights in hopes of sleeping with her. But his sense of honor did not permit him any actions in pursuit of his reveries except a dreamy gaze that he delivered with fidelity, a disconcerting gaze that Zannuba—with all her experience—found strange and off-putting, and before which she stood incapable of taking any compensatory measures. And so, in the end, she was forced to set him down carefully in that quiet region reserved for things deserving of sympathy. Real compassion, for even if he was not the knight she had hoped for, he was not just anyone, some ordinary fellow she could pass right by without sensing her own femininity to the fullest. All of her forays were blessed with a certain bodily frankness that went so far—sometimes—as to do violence to proprietary boundaries. He was the one man who respected her body and treated it with the necessary and proper reverence.

Ustadh Ramadan was a poet and at the same time was no poet. The extent to which he *might well* be a poet of talent was cancelled out exactly by the limits of possibility, which meant he was categorically and fundamentally not a poet, never had been, and never would be. He himself would speak of the great import of poetry and the pressing need Life has of it, with the same level of passion that enveloped him on those occasions when he acknowledged that poetry had ruined and destroyed his life. He went back and forth on this for years on end, and his vacillation found resolution only in the time lost and wasted, devoted to poetry. He was successful, materially successful, in enticing a knot of literature's young to flock to him for a weekly poetry salon that he held at home, which he considered a fitting compensation for those many long wasted years, and because of which he was forced to endure the hardship of scoldings from the Beauty Queen of Beni Sweif, who in the nature of things had not fully comprehended his literary prowess.

His salon occurred every Friday. At the conclusion of one of them he returned to the Beauty Queen of Beni Sweif, hoping she would not give him the usual lashing. He was in a state of trance brought on by the kernel of an idea for a new ode. He leaned against the bed and started to declaim its opening line in a self-assured voice:

I pen joy, weeping and moaning I record
With tambourine or ode
And my shadow over the water's surface slides on

Overcome by the beauty of the lines he'd thought up, the Prof
scurried to his desk, but the pen and the stark whiteness of the
paper staunched the onrush of his thoughts and he went back to
bed. The creative spell was at its apogee, and he asked the Beauty
Queen of Beni Sweif to follow him around with the cassette
recorder. It was an idea that had been with him for a long time,
tugging at him, but he had never implemented it: to record his
poems rather than writing them out. For it was his conviction
that the pen hobbled poetry with excessive intellectualism, pre-
cluding a state of madness for which poetry cried out. And while
the Beauty Queen was searching for a blank cassette befitting the
madness of her husband, his head dropped.

Ustadh Ramadan died, passing on in his disciples' absence.
When the news came to me I felt even though he was a run-of-
the-mill or more precisely negligible friend, a kind of disorienta-
tion at his loss. Or perhaps what I experienced was the collapse
of those secure fortress walls that had previously saved me from
facing my own failures and disappointments. In some way his
presence had given me a sense of security, even though I don't
remember actually ever making an effort to see him, not even
once. Prof Ramadan was a lot like me. He was in a sense a failure.
And for the sake of one's own self-assurance it is more critical
to make friends with others who are failures too, than it is to
preserve friendships with people who can't stop stringing up
one success after another. For if a friend is your mirror, really

and truly, then the friend who's a flop is the closest you can get to having a finely ground glass that gives you confidence about the worth of your actions and displays before you, in all detail, your successes, despite their rarity and feebleness. The successful friend, on the other hand, raises to your face a frame that frustrates you with the unwinding reel of his unending successes.

Yes, Ustadh Ramadan died. Even in the presence of every sort of devastating emotion, one can still admit that his death—on the level of literary diffusion—was better than his life ever had been. One of the better-known newspapers voluntarily eulogized him with detailed reportage of his life and literary legacies, describing him as "the major poet" and locating in his death an opportune occasion for bewailing the corruption of literary life in Egypt, offering as evidence the neglect of towering figures like him. Likewise, Ustadh Ramadan's students collaborated to produce a heavy volume with a fancy cover illustration taken from an old photo in which he appeared all smiles and beaming modesty. On the back cover they put an affecting declaration in which he introduced himself by saying, "I am a man who writes poetry and whom no one knows. In the sixties I had not yet matured and I was dissatisfied, more or less, with what I wrote. I feared exposure to the wounding arrows of literary criticism. But these days—ever since I have been wedded to poetry in an eternal bond—I am thinking about bringing out my first collection, although the fact that I am unknown in literary circles pains me."

This book brought together his most distinguished odes and words of elegy that he fully deserved.

Petalled Remnants
on the Grave of the Noble Poet . . .

For it is truly as though from the wondrous age of the great he emerged. With all of the noble sentiments was he adorned, and with all honorable generous qualities he lived and gave of himself. He was not a poet who composed poetry—only; verily, he was a human being who bore his sweet humanity wherever he alighted, exuding to those around him warmth, affection, love, and that pure smile, in any collocation among which he collocated. And his poetry was a portion of his soul, in which lay his strength, his gravity, and his everlasting youth.

His features underwent no variance throughout the entire period of my acquaintance with him: a beaming face on a slender body that told you that you were standing before a man who gave off the flavor of history and exemplified its towering presence. In him were concentrated the experience and trials of his days; lo, time itself ushered him toward this mode of being, this formation that graced him. His grandeur preceded him in the eyes of others, such that it ill behooved a person to treat him in any ordinary way. Your imagination would inevitably engrave his image—as you sat in his presence—as that of a wise man from the days of the Pharaohs or a poet from the noble ranks of the ancient Arabs, those giants, indeed those virile stallions, of poetry. His elocutions were magniloquent, his utterances amiable and poignant, his very presence the stuff of authority. He shall remain always in our consciences and consciousness the epitome of chivalry, nobility, and eloquent expression; and if the great poet Shawqi were among us today, then truly a tear would grace his cheek in heartfelt poetic display. God give him mercy, and let us mourn our loss in him and embrace him as a symbol of the noble literary knight.

The knight has descended from his mount. The time has come for him to rest after his arduous trial. Ah, towering knight, slender as the obelisks of the ancient Egyptians, ah, our knight with his feet firmly implanted in the depths of this land, your noble head gazing down from the heavens, Time was not compassionate, Time did not extend itself enough, for you to now withdraw from our happy collocation, to extinguish whatever light it enjoyed. . . . Time, time, it was not Time.

And, furthermore. His classical insight into the concept of the contemplative philosopher-poet, alone with no company in his ivory tower contemplating reality as it unfolds played a most decisive role in transforming his struggle between two paths in life, indeed two ways of Life, reforming it as the contradiction between the man of reality immersed wholly in politics and the movement of the street and the poet of sensitivity who succeeds in contemplating reality only to the extent that he remains distant from it. And the scale tipped always toward a form of reconciliation and adjustment even as the needle of reconciliation swung on, and on, between the two contradictory positions that defined the essence of this man, this Poet.

Physicians alone take the price in advance. And Ramadan was no physician. For he waited until life drew to its end. A lifetime little suffices in this nation that we may acquire his beneficence. The poet passed on, erect. And though I love him and esteem his noble being yet I do not aspire, ever, nor can I aspire, ever, to be his like. A heavy burden would it be indeed: that his tragedy would come to pass twice.

The Beauty Queen of Beni Sweif accepted the efforts of the departed poet's students with obvious disdain. When one of them leaned over to whisper diffidently in her ear that printing the volume had cost three thousand pounds, she took the news as yet another disaster that had descended onto her head, and beat on her breast as widows do. *"Yaa kharaaaabiiii! Yaa* disaaaaster my dis-aaaaster has arrived! His household was not the one that most deserved this!"

The manifestations of her grief for the poet himself were more practical and down-to-earth: she kept them to a single wailed phrase, to the effect that she *no longer had a place in this wide world outside of this house after his passing.* It was an ordinary phrase that all women utter as a matter of course when they've lost their husbands. But it was a sign of things to come in the case of the Beauty Queen. The apartment was registered in the name of the Prof, and naturally after his passing she was imminently to be thrown out. Except that her scheme succeeded. She came out of the whole affair triumphant, with a license she had not even dreamed of. Abu Gamal's voice was hoarse as he spoke. "Now you just make yourself at home. This house, my girl, treat it as your home, *ya bint in-naas,* and if the wide world doesn't bear your tribulations, my fine girl, why, I'll mount you atop my own head, I will, cross my heart."

15

Immediately facing my apartment's balcony is the window of a single room that is the sum total of the beneficences of this world remaining to a certain elderly married pair. The husband went on pension a quarter-century ago, while the wife was perfectly content, having exhausted four husbands before him. A pair still affectionate despite the accumulation of decades, their sole activity was to gaze steadfastly at each other. It's true that they don't give the slightest verbal expression to this love, but consistently and reliably—though at varying intervals—they energize it by exchanging a fortifying smile accompanied by a sure nod of the head. It's a historic and profoundly rooted smile that gave life to their lips for the first time the night of the wedding, which was without a doubt a felicitous one.

Mornings they sit in front of the house, while for the remainder of the twenty-four hours they're at the window. This post-morning session not only is the longer and quieter one but also has the added element of a new technique, which is to extend their necks as far as necessary to take in the entire street from top to bottom. Two small and stiffly fixed skulls shift with a routinized and carefully controlled movement as their eyes gawk at an oncoming figure whom they can't see clearly and who never actually arrives. At the dawn call to prayer the large head—the *head* head—jerks suddenly, as the dignity of an individual with a sense of his own (exalted) place in the world takes over. The response to this involves not only the head of the devoted wife but indeed the heads of the entire street as well. Having faithfully and assiduously performed the dawn prayer for thirty-eight years, the husband hopes fervently that God will give his life a little extension so that he can round things off at a full forty years of prayer. Such devotion and longing go into this hope that I'm compelled to support him by adding a plea from where I stand: may his abiding wish be granted.

The dawn prayer has its miraculous blessings of which he is well aware, and from his position at the window he strives valiantly to make them available to all. First he shouts to the residents of his building, then to those of mine, and finally to the street's entire population, but always one by one. His is the loud call of the fervid, of the one who knows that he—yes, he—is capable of acting. It's the bellow of a man who has found in the religious occasion a unique witness to his existence, and the determinative dividing point between his life and the end of it.

The two fear death. Not death itself, for death is a certainty and they're pretty sure that life has exceeded its prescribed limit by now. What they fear is the fragrance of death, the rot one expects to smell coming from a body that is dead and on its own. Even a body that seems no more than skin stretched over a bony extent must inevitably disintegrate. This is what terrifies them: that the two of them will depart this life in one lone room and people won't have the slightest idea until the anticipated smells start to spread, that scandalous odor! If a person can be so shame-faced about a passing wind that suddenly explodes out of his innards, what about his whole body *turning into* an odor, nothing but an odor, an indecent disgraceful embarrassing smell that will erase all sorts of things and cancel out the honorable positions he took, enduring the weight of them simply for the sake of being remembered by folks after his death. In fact, it will effectively condense his life, which was long and rich, into a measly bother wrapped up in the strained sympathy folks feel about his body rotting with no one around to know about it. This would be a sheer scandal. And so the pair combats it daily by shouting, "Wake up, folks! Wake up, dawn is HERE and life is passing BY!" They fight the looming scandal with their silence, too. Sometimes he runs an experiment on his neighbors by deliberately postponing the roar that will shout the street into collective prayer. He hides his head close beneath the window to await the result. The moment someone successfully glances up at the window with a surprised inquiry—"Hey, Hagg, you oversleeping today?"—he springs to life like a father whose son has just passed a tough and vital exam.

16

Flaming, Nada stalked up the stairs to her uncle in the chicken coop and announced the news. "Sayf's bolted! Did it again! All night long and he never did come to bed, and this morning there's no sign of him!"

Sayf did go out most nights, and sometimes he was gone for hours at a time. He'd hunt up whatever easy cash he could find and go out on the town. Not anything to speak of—a couple of pounds, maybe three, often just the last half-pound in Nada's possession. But it was enough to set him dousing his hair with a watercress preparation, accentuating his lips and eyebrows, and getting his face just right with the help of a mask, whereupon he'd stuff his hands into his pants and roam the streets, his mouth giving lyrical shape to some emotive tune. He'd say he was going out to get fresh air far away from the house's choking environment. His brothers, under Gamal's leadership, muttered that he was hunting customers. But Nada wasn't exaggerating her anxiety and irritation, because on this occasion he was later than usual; he was *late late late*. And he hadn't even snatched the spending money from beneath the pillow, as he usually did. The timing made it even more agonizing: only the week before, a curfew had been imposed on him for throwing himself into the Nile

from the nearby Bridge of the Amply Blessed in a famous incident the details of which the official and mainstream newspapers
made sure to transmit, though the item was tucked away in their
"Anecdotes and Oddities" columns.

Abu Gamal gave Nada his immediate attention, because the
boy was mad crazy and would do such a thing. He expressed his
concern by jumping onto his bicycle and turning the handlebars
toward the station, which was the preferred and ideal site for
Sayf's sacrosanct pleasure-seeking outings. Gamal, meanwhile,
was on a nerve-wracking expedition with the Counselor to return all of that water under the bridge to its normal course. Nada
felt she had wound up her role in the crisis in exemplary fashion
by broadcasting the news, though her face retained the traces of
affect worthy of a wife who has lost her husband, and she poured
her remaining energies into nursing the baby. Um Gamal found
in the situation a perfect opportunity to wail and moan and dis-
tribute her curses equally and evenly among all the women of the
house with special attention to Gamal's wife and cousin, Hanan.
Amer, sitting with Adil in front of the house, went on rolling his
bango joint, ignoring his mother's screeching. When an obviously embarrassed Adil told him what all the noise was about,
Amer found his appropriate response by commenting, "That
daughter of a whore wants a funeral with all the trappings, all the
women slapping their cheeks, and she knows better than anyone
that the son of a dirty whore will come home like the shoe you
wear." And no sooner did he take a deep drag and say smugly to
Adil, "Have some, man," than he was able to add, "And now here
he is, slinking back like a dog." Adil turned to find Sayf standing
right behind him, smiling. And before anyone could start in on
the usual questions or the anticipated scolding, Sayf startled
everyone—or, say, he slapped a bridle over their tongues—with

a truly alarming response. "I was at Granny's. I cried and cried, sitting right there by her side, all day long, and when she saw I was tired out she said to me, 'Go home, Sayf. Go on home, son, before they pen you up again.'"

Before anyone could jump in to ask after her conditions in the House of Eternity, Umm Gamal changed the subject to her conditions in the Lower House. "God be merciful, she was a good woman," and hugged Sayf, adding with genuine sorrow, "She called you, son. When she was dying she told me to watch over you specially."

Fleeing to Granny when the world closes in was not a strategy unique to Sayf. All his siblings did that, and first among them was the thinker, Gamal. The sole text he had disseminated through publication, in his entire life, took her as its theme. He published it on her grave. He bought a polished marble chunk, erected it as a gravestone, and engraved on it: *Everyone has a special legend around which to weave their history. The average person takes pride in this, ornamenting the story of his life with all the heroisms he aspires to, and with it he assuages the ways life has burned him. And "Naqawa" is our legend . . . our undying legend.* He signed with his pen name, "Gamal Abu Naqawa."

She was their mother and their father. Her husband had left her in search of glory in other wombs, in search of a boy to carry his name. She found in Abu Gamal and Um Gamal fitting recompense, or a fine opportunity for revenge, obedient instruments to bring to fruition the glory that her body had been unable to achieve.

It wasn't a difficult project. Um Gamal was her daughter; all she had to do was to launch an exploratory survey to select another son, a good pliable young man from a family that would counteract the venerable roots of her own, a low family, a family with no past nor any future either, a youth whose ambitions reached only as far as rich, fatty foods and a pack of Cleopatra Supers every morning. Most important: one who saw no glory and honor in sons. In this sense precisely, Abu Gamal was an exemplary choice. To this day he was seeking, bemused, a decent *reason why that woman had so much love for the little buggers.*

Every baby that came rolling out she added to the two children she already had, Abu Gamal and Um Gamal. For every little fellow she sketched out the future of his life. Gamal was her great joy, the first child to give her that awesome sense of possession, so strong it made her tremble. No sooner did he slide out of Um Gamal's womb than she fell onto—or let's say she swooped down on—his member with hot, hysterical kisses, historic kisses. For years afterward, without showing the slightest embarrassment, she planted those little kisses, in the same spot, right out in public. In her final throes, her only hope—one denied to her by the sacred hush of a deathbed—was to plant on his manhood a final kiss.

With Salah, Granny succeeded—through the good offices of her siblings—in getting him on the soccer team at Zamalek Sporting Club. Gamal she schemed and strategized to get made a counselor like her brother. Sayf left her bemused because his talents were so many and so varied: she could see him as an actor, or then as a musician, or then again as a public relations man . . . but in the end she left him confused and did not steer him in the appropriate direction. . . . Naqawa died. She died and put everyone in a quandary. The children suddenly realized that in fact they were obliged to love and obey parents who were not her, while Sakina and Abd al-Halim found themselves suddenly playing mother and father—truly being Abu Gamal and um Gamal to boys who had been like their own sibs.

17

Finally Amer put in an appearance.

He was dangling from the chicken house wall, and his form became visible in the light shaft. All the waiting and watching had worn me out. My plots to conceal myself had succeeded only in magnifying my fear of them and their doubts about me. Abu Gamal himself announced flat out that he suspected I was up to something, and the live wiring with which I had reinforced the battlements of my apartment began to scare me, morphing into a time bomb primed to explode at any moment. So I decided to execute an ultimate plan and be done with it all and leave the protection of my apartment to the observant eye of God. Therefore, as Abu Gamal was holding his daily council in front of the house, I announced that I would be joining my wife in the village. I had said good-bye to her a few days before, and as she climbed into the bus by herself I felt a real sense of relief that almost convinced me there was no point in going through with the plan. Amer wasn't even around. But I figured that colliding with Zannuba on the stairs as I lugged my suitcase down served him ample notice that my apartment was empty in anticipation of his visit.

I set off on an all-inclusive and unhurried tour around Manshiya Nasir, launching my little expedition by taking in a little air at the filtration plant, then pondering the strategic point from which the Leader Gamal Abd al-Nasir had waved his hand in that historic gesture of his. I wrapped it up by sitting at the café until about midnight. Then I walked back. The rectangular plot in front of the building had held onto some of its earlier pristine appearance. At the center and slightly toward the entrance were four small holes, but deepish ones, suggesting that Abu Gamal's chair had been vacated only a short time before. The stairwell light was out and overall the building was enjoying a moment of calm very like the magical early dawn of those nights on which Zannuba and more precisely Sayf had come to my apartment.

I crept up to my apartment and opened the door with extreme caution, just as any professional thief would do. No sooner had I shut the door than I was overwhelmed by a sense of the hopelessness of these onerous security efforts, and a certainty that all members of the tribe of Abu Gamal were watching me like a character in a superficial novel or an easy prey that there's no doubt will fall. But now, here was Amer's body, writhing through the light shaft, making for my apartment exactly as I had surmised and planned for.

I didn't feel at all malicious toward him. Sometimes I had frightened myself with the hunch that the electric current I had engineered with my own hand would strike him. But I thought he deserved the work of making a fitting ending to this novel, which would also put limits on my fear. *Sometimes a foolhardy rush toward the place where danger lurks is the best way to dispel your fear.* That's what Gamal wrote. I was somewhat like a hunter: usually he doesn't hate his prey, but he's eager all the same for it to fall into his trap. It's true that at various miserable points I had felt

like letting go, but I always gained the upper hand over my antagonist by imagining that I had really killed him. I imposed a future on myself in which, as with the past, there was no turning
back, no way to change one's mind.

I couldn't decide where I could best hide to make it appear
that I was (legally) innocent of all ensuing events. It was the first
time I'd found my apartment truly small. Two adjoining rooms
plus a bathroom with a foyer that I'd always considered pretty
roomy as a kitchen.

In the end I hurried into the bedroom, since the window allowed me—despite the annoyance of the wardrobe, which got in
the way—to follow Amer's efforts closely. At first I wasn't able to
see him, and I supposed that he had grown wise to my presence.
But suddenly two bare feet and two hands came into sight,
swinging in the light shaft. So he had definitely succeeded in
leaving the wall of the chicken coop behind. Now his hands
were clutching the rim of the window of Salah's bathroom on
the fourth floor, and he left it to his feet to open my bathroom
window. Two feet lost in the expanse of the light shaft, and in fact
they were so unmatched to this mission that it frustrated me. In
this innocent position, he could fall and shatter his bones without any need for my scheme. It would be preferable for him to
support himself with one foot pressing against one of the light
shaft's walls and the other on the facing wall, and then resume his
descent until his head was level with the window of my bathroom. Then he could dive easily into my apartment. Especially
since the light shaft was exactly one and a quarter meters wide.

He rested his left foot on the window, and when he applied
pressure, the foot slipped and he really did fall—almost. That
gave me a scare. I thought about tiptoeing over to the window

and adjusting the position of his feet to be right above the un-coated electric wire. But at last one of his two idiotic feet hit one side of the window and it swung open. He put the other foot down next to it and lowered his whole body. The wire leaped and pounced just like any other murderer, and the minute he shifted his feet, preparing to jump inside my apartment, I heard a shriek and he disappeared from my sight. I changed my viewing position. He bumped against the opposite wall of the light shaft before plunging into its depths, already a stiff corpse. I was at the bathroom window, swinging between two contradictory emo-tions: pride, as prey that had managed to defend itself fiercely; and fear and regret, as a killer anticipating the miseries of an in-evitable coming revenge. Abu Gamal noticed me. . . .

Because he was positioned in the stairwell apartment—in the Doctoress's place—and also because he was positioned as boss of the building, Abu Gamal was the first to take note of the fall of Amer. His sentiments were ordinary ones for a judicious father who construed his son's fall as a natural outcome of his excessive drug consumption. But when he discovered that Amer had been cut down by an exposed live wire he remembered catching a glimpse of me. . . .

He saw me clearly. It would be shameful to throw me out of the building. And he didn't dare admit that his son's blood, as it were, hung around my neck. So he confronted me with a look that skillfully blended stout respect with a baffled worry as to how he would select the perfect ending, one that would be just right for me.